Sage is in love with Reece, and he knows Reece is in love with him, even though Reece does his best to hide it. That's what being an empath means for Sage—being able to feel other people's emotions even if he doesn't want to. It also means hiding what he is so people can't take advantage of him like his alpha did, and now, he doesn't know how to tell Reece—or if he should.

Carey is in Rosewood to protect two unicorn shifters. As a phoenix shifter, it's an easy job for him, and he's looking forward to discovering the town and the pack. He didn't expect to meet his mate, but he's over the moon. He doesn't even care that Sage is in love with another guy. If anything, he's happy about it. Who wouldn't want two boyfriends, right?

Reece has been mourning since he lost his mate and their little girl. He's been in love with Sage for almost as long as he's been back in Rosewood, but he's never done anything about it. He never planned to, either.

But then Carey barges into his and Sage's life.

Reece doesn't know if he can be with two men, especially since Sage and Carey share a mate bond, but it's either try or be alone for the rest of his life—and he doesn't know if he can do that, either.

Rise from the Ashes
Copyright © 2020 Catherine Lievens
ISBN: 978-1-4874-2849-5
Cover art by Angela Waters

Published by eXtasy Books Inc or
Devine Destinies, an imprint of eXtasy Books Inc

Look for us online at:
www.eXtasybooks.com or www.devinedestinies.com

Rise from the Ashes
Legendary Shifters 3

By

Catherine Lievens

Chapter One

Sage was in love with Reece.

He'd been in love with Reece since what felt like forever, even though he'd only been with the pack a few years. Reece had burrowed his way under Sage's skin, though. It had always been that way, since the first time they saw each other, and Sage wasn't sure what to do.

He knew Reece wanted him just as much. He could feel it. That was one of the curses that came with Sage's gift.

He wasn't a unicorn shifter. He couldn't heal. Instead, he was an empath. He could feel what other people felt, and that made his life hell. He was used to it, and living with the pack had helped, because it didn't have many members and no one thought anything of Sage mostly keeping to his house and the forest, but he still could feel what Reece felt for him every time he was with him, along with everything else he felt, which was why he hadn't talked to him about it.

He knew Reece loved him, but he was also sad and wary, and he kept his distance. Sage might be able to feel his emotions, but he didn't know *why* Reece felt the way he felt, and he wasn't about to ask. If Reece wanted to tell him, he knew where to find him. He would come.

Except he hadn't, not yet. Sage had stopped hoping he would. He'd stopped hoping there ever would be more between them than friendship.

"Sage? Are you okay?" Reece asked, waving his hand in front of Sage's face.

Sage blinked and took a sip of soda to make it look like he

knew what he was doing when he didn't. "I'm fine."

"You are? Because it doesn't look like it." Reece leaned closer. "What's going on? Do you need anything?"

And that was one of the reasons Sage loved Reece. He was so caring, even though they were nothing to each other except neighbors. Reece was always there for Sage, whatever Sage needed. The same could be said about the rest of the pack, or at least, most of them, but Sage only had feelings for Reece.

And he didn't know what to do about them.

Sage knew something was wrong. He also knew that there would never be anything between them, even though he couldn't say why.

"Are you sure you're okay?" Reece continued. "Because it doesn't look like it."

Sage didn't know what to tell Reece. It wasn't like he could explain what his real problem was. That would probably send him running, and that was the last thing Sage needed.

He forced himself to smile. "I'm fine. How about you? How do you feel about your best friend finding his mate?"

Reece blinked. "How should I feel about that?"

"I don't know. It probably isn't easy for you, considering you and Frederic seemed to be attached at the hip until recently."

Reece wrinkled his nose. "That's not true."

"But it is true that you're best friends."

"That doesn't mean we were attached at the hip. We're both adults. We both had other things to do. Besides, I spent years away from him and the pack. I can deal with this. Hell, I've dealt with worse."

Sage raised his free hand. "Sorry. I didn't mean to offend you."

Reece shook his head. "You didn't offend me. I just wasn't aware that people thought we were so close. We *are* close, but we can survive without the other."

Sage was sorry he'd asked. "Don't mind me. I was trying to make conversation, and I'm clearly not good at it."

Reece opened his mouth to speak, but just then someone approached them rapidly and Sage turned to look at him, puzzled. The man exuded a series of emotions Sage couldn't read, or rather, they were too muddled for him to read them.

The man—Sage knew he was one of the twins who'd arrived to help protect the pack, and more importantly, Toby and his brother Sam—held a hand out to Sage.

Sage blinked and reached out to take it, thinking the man wanted to shake it, but instead, he pulled Sage closer, so close that his nose brushed against the skin of Sage's neck as he leaned against him.

"What the fuck do you think you're doing?" Reece snapped. He grabbed Sage's arm and pulled him back, and to Sage's relief, the man let him go.

"I'm Carey," the twin said.

"I'm Sage, and this is Reece," Sage said.

"And you haven't told us what the fuck you were doing," Reece said, his voice hard.

Sage wasn't surprised to find Reece overprotective. He always was. That didn't mean there was anything else to it, though.

Carey's smile widened, which puzzled Sage. He was so used to being able to read people's emotions that the other man's feelings left him unsteady.

"He's my mate," Carey declared.

There was a moment of silence, and Sage tried to make sense of what Carey had said. He had to be talking about him, right? That was the only thing that made sense, since he'd pulled Sage close to sniff him.

"I'm sorry?" Reece asked, his voice slightly softer, hurt.

Sage's chest tightened painfully. It was hard to breathe.

He hadn't expected to meet his mate. He knew he had a

mate out there somewhere, but what were the odds that he would find the man? On the other hand, he never expected anything to happen between him and Reece, so did that really matter? He and Reece might be in love with each other, but Carey was Sage's mate. Sage should give him a chance.

"I said, he's my mate," Carey repeated.

Sage hoped he *could* give Carey a chance. He didn't know Carey, but he was sure the man was a good person. He also couldn't continue pining after Reece, no matter how much it hurt—or rather, *because* of how much it hurt.

"Is that true, Sage?" Reece asked.

Sage blinked. Of course Reece wanted to know. Sage could feel what Reece felt, and it was a mess of emotions—pain, confusion, frustration.

Love shouldn't hurt this much.

"I would have to come closer to be sure. I didn't expect this to happen, so I didn't smell Carey when he pulled me close."

Carey grinned. "Feel free to feel or smell me up anytime you want to."

Sage would have rolled his eyes if Reece hadn't been so angry. He understood his anger, though. Even though Reece had never had any intention of being more than a friend to Sage, he couldn't help how he felt. Emotions and what Reece *thought* was the right thing to do didn't mesh, and that was what Sage had had to deal with ever since he and Reece had met.

Sage stepped closer to Carey. "I'm going to smell you now," he said.

Carey was still grinning like a loon.

Sage knew what Carey was feeling—a slight confusion, but most of all, elation, happiness. Whatever else Carey thought about this, he was ecstatic about having found his mate. He might not know Sage, but there was determination in his feelings, and Sage knew that whatever happened, Carey wouldn't give up easily. He had that stubborn streak in him, and while that should have frightened Sage a least a little, it didn't.

It felt good to be wanted for once.

Sage leaned closer, and even though he didn't stick his nose against Carey's neck like Carey had done with him, he was close enough to know that Carey was right.

They were mates.

Sage took a step back. "He is."

Reece was still holding Sage's arm, and his hand squeezed almost to the point of pain. Sage didn't say anything, though. This was the most Reece had felt when it came to him and this kind of thing, and for a moment, it felt good. It gave Sage hope that Reece might finally see the truth, that he might take a step closer.

But of course, he didn't. If anything, he became more distant. "So he's your mate? Really?"

Sage nodded. "Really. I'm sorry."

Reece took his head. "You have nothing to be sorry about."

Sage wasn't sure that was true, but there was nothing he could do to change the situation—and he wasn't sure he would if there was.

Carey was over the moon happy. The last thing he'd expected was to meet his mate during a party with the pack he and Lennox were helping.

He'd thought this job would be like all the others—in and out as fast as they could so they could move on to the next job. He'd suspected it would be different as soon as he'd met the alpha and the alpha's mate, but this beat all of that.

Carey had met his mate. That meant that unless something went really wrong, the pack would be his home. His and his brother's. That was all Carey had ever wanted for both of them, and he couldn't stop smiling. He was pretty sure it made him look like an idiot, but he didn't even care.

He'd met his mate.

The other man, the one Sage had called Reece, frowned. It was more like a glare, really, but it was obvious he was trying very hard not to show what was going on his head. To Carey, he looked angry and sad, but Carey had no clue why. He didn't know enough about the pack and the dynamics, but that would have to change.

Maybe Reece was jealous. Carey suspected there was something between him and Sage, and that was fine with him. He was getting two guys instead of one. Who wouldn't be happy about that?

Reece finally let go of Sage. "Well, Sage, I'm happy for you. You deserve this." He gestured toward a house in the distance. "I'm going to go. I have things to do."

Sage's expression twisted. "Wait. You don't have to go."

"I do. He's your mate. You two should get to know each other."

There was a barely repressed rage on Reece's face now, and Carey was even more confused. He watched Reece walk away, then turned to look at Sage. Sage remained focused on Reece — something was clearly going on between them.

Carey half expected Sage to be angry at him for barging into his conversation with Reece. It wouldn't be the first time something like that happened, and Carey was used to it. He knew he should think before he did things, but he always acted on instinct. Lennox was the twin who was reflective and took his time. Carey was the opposite, and while sometimes, it led to trouble, most of the time, he was more than happy to continue behaving the way he did.

He just hoped it hadn't messed up his chance with his mate and their boyfriend.

Sage turned toward Carey.

Carey held his breath. Was he about to be yelled at? Sage was obviously distraught.

But Sage schooled his expression. "I'm sorry for how Reece acted."

Carey cocked his head. "What are you sorry for?" Even if Reece was angry or offended, Sage shouldn't be the one apologizing.

"It was a surprise for both of us. We didn't expect to meet — well, *I* didn't expect to meet my mate today. I'm sorry for the way he talked to you. He shouldn't have."

Carey raised a hand, and Sage snapped his mouth shut. "You don't have to apologize."

"I know, Reece should be the one apologizing, but —"

"No, he shouldn't. I don't expect an explanation or an apology from anyone. Relax. You don't have to freak out. I'm not angry or offended or whatever you're thinking. Take a deep breath."

Sage obeyed. He sucked in a breath, then another, and looked at Carey again. "So. You said your name is Carey, and I know you're one of the phoenix shifter twins who arrived recently. I wasn't there during the confrontation with the Springfield pack envoy, though."

"I would have noticed you if you'd been there," Carey pointed out. He knew he would have, even though he'd been busy worrying about the confrontation. Well, not exactly worrying. He wasn't the worrying kind of guy. That was Lennox. But he'd been looking forward to the confrontation, and he hadn't been sorry. He also hadn't been sorry that he'd almost burned the envoy to ashes. That had been a fun bit.

Sage rubbed his face. Carey didn't like how shaken he was, even though he understood why. It had to be a huge change, going from having a boyfriend to having your mate standing in front of you, telling you that the two of you belong together. There was something Sage didn't understand, though, and Carey needed to let him know before anything else happened.

Carey opened his mouth to speak, but then Sage said, "I need time."

Carey took a moment to think about his answer. Usually, he would have just blurted out whatever went through his mind, but Sage wasn't just a guy. He was Carey's mate, and Carey needed to make sure he wouldn't fuck this up by acting on instinct. "Is Reece your boyfriend?"

Sage frowned. "I just told you I need time. Why are you asking that?"

"Because I'd like to know. And yes, I heard you. You need time, and I'm more than happy to give that to you. You can take all the time you need. I'm not going to force you into anything, or to rush you."

Sage shook his head. "That's not what I was saying."

"I know it's not. I just wanted to make things clear. Which is why I mentioned Reece. Is he your boyfriend?"

"No."

That confused Carey even more. "Are you sure? Because he reacted as if you are."

"It's complicated."

"I bet it is. It was obvious both of you have feelings for each other, though, so I want you to know that I don't care. It doesn't matter to me."

Sage narrowed his eyes. "What do you mean? Are you giving me your blessing to be with Reece?"

"If that's what you want, sure. But that's not what I was trying to say."

"What were you trying to say, then?"

"That while you're my mate, I wouldn't mind both of us having a boyfriend, too. I'm not stuck up, and while I don't believe in cheating, this *wouldn't* be cheating."

"I don't understand what's going on."

Carey needed to be even more precise so they didn't misunderstand what was happening. "I want to be with you. You're my mate, and neither of us will ever find something like this again. But I wouldn't have asked you and Reece to break up if you'd been together. I believe in being faithful when it comes to relationships, but that doesn't mean there can only be two people in our relationship. I've been with two people at the same time, and it works, as long as the three of us are okay with it and talk. That's what I was trying to say."

Sage looked confused, and Carey hoped he'd gotten through.

"I'm going to have to think about this," Sage finally said. "I'm sorry. I told you I needed time."

"And I get that. Take as much time as you need, and the same goes for Reece. But if you see him, please tell him. I don't expect the two of you to break up, or whatever you might do since you just said you're not together. I don't want the two of you to grow apart. I'm not jealous, and I would be more than happy to be in a relationship with both you and Reece. That's all."

Carey hoped he wouldn't regret this. He knew most people thought he was weird, and maybe he was. Maybe he shouldn't be this relaxed when it came to who his mate was and who he was with, but he didn't care what other people thought. He truly believed that throuples could work. He believed in being loved twice as much, and in giving twice the love. Love wasn't a fixed emotion. It expanded, it grew, and Carey wanted Sage and Reece to know that.

And fuck what anyone else might think.

Reece stumbled home. He couldn't remember a time when he'd been so angry and disappointed, even though he shouldn't be. He shouldn't feel this way. He wasn't allowed to, and that was his own fault.

He was the one who'd always kept Sage at arm's length. He was the one who'd ignored all the times Sage tried to get closer. He'd also ignored the signs that Sage felt more than friendship for him, and this was the result.

And he knew it was better this way.

Carey was Sage's mate. He and Sage belong together, and Reece didn't have a say in that, no matter how angry he was. He shouldn't be, though. He'd had plenty of occasions to be with Sage. He and Sage could have been together almost since the beginning when Sage first arrived. But instead, Reece had made sure they were only friends.

And now he'd lost Sage forever.

He slammed his front door shut and leaned against it, closing his eyes and trying to breathe through the anger and the pain.

He knew it was better that way, and not just because Carey and Sage were mates. It was better because of his own past. It was better because he couldn't fall in love again. He couldn't let that happen, not the way it had happened before. He wouldn't be able to stand a loss of that enormity again, and that was why he'd ignored Sage's shy openings.

He wasn't sure he could watch Sage run off with Carey, though.

Eventually, it would happen. Reece could imagine how things would go — Sage would try talking to him at least a few times, possibly more. He would try to explain what had happened with Carey, and he would apologize. That was just how Sage was. He always apologized, even when he didn't have anything to apologize for.

So he would try to make Reece see that if Reece wanted, he could ignore the bond he shared with Carey. Reece was almost a hundred percent sure that would happen, and Reece would tell him that it didn't matter, that he should focus on

Carey because Carey was his mate and they belonged together. Sage wouldn't push. He never did. That was why he and Reece were still only friends. Everyone knew there was more than that between them, or at least, that there had been. That was over now, though.

Everything was over.

Reece didn't want to have to watch Sage and Carey be happy together. The instinct to pack and leave was strong. He might have, if the pack wasn't his home.

But it was.

Reece's past had shown him that, and he knew things wouldn't go well if he left, no matter how much he wanted to. He would have to face the pain and deal with it. He was used to doing that anyway. This wouldn't any different.

A knock on the front door made him jump. He didn't want to talk to whoever was on the other side of it, even though there was a strong possibility that someone was Sage. Reece decided to ignore it and stayed as still as he could, but he should have known better.

"I know you're in there," Frederic said.

Reece should have known Frederic would come by. He was Reece's best friend, and more than once, he'd asked Reece why he didn't talk to Sage, why the two of them weren't together. He knew what Reece had gone through, but he couldn't understand why Reece couldn't have anything with Sage or anyone else ever again. No one could.

"I saw you walk home. Why aren't you at the party? What happened with Sage and Carey? I saw the three of you talk, then you left, and you looked angry. Did Carey say something?"

Reece knew Frederic wasn't going anywhere. Until Reece opened his door, he would stay there, flinging questions and waiting for answers. Not getting them wasn't going to deter him. It never did.

Reece sighed heavily, then pushed away from the door and opened it. He glared at Frederic, but Frederic ignored him. He already had more questions. "Was Carey rude to you? Because from what I know, he's not a bad guy, just weird. You probably shouldn't be offended by whatever he told you, but if it was that bad, you need to talk to him, or better yet, Camden. He'll tell Carey to shut the fuck up or something like that."

Reece crossed his arms over his chest. "Why do you think he was rude to me?"

Frederic arched a brow. "Remember that bit about you stomping away looking angry? *That's* why."

Reece needed to make a decision. He could tell Frederic what had happened, or he could act as if everything was fine. He doubted Frederic would believe him, but maybe he wouldn't push.

Hope was the last thing to die and all that.

Reece shook his head and took a step back so Frederic could come in. "You should go back to the party," he said.

"I'm not going back until you talk to me. I've had enough of this island bullshit. Since you've come back, you've isolated yourself even more, and I don't like it. It's been years, Reece. Talk to me. Please."

Reece couldn't. He'd been back seven years, and he'd kept the pain and memories close to his heart. He didn't want that to change. He couldn't allow that to happen because it would make his daily life close to impossible to live. He needed to be able to ignore what had happened to go on. He'd told Frederic once when he was drunk, and he'd promised himself he would never mention it again, to anyone.

"Nothing happened with Carey and me. He came over to us, told Sage they're mates, and that was that."

Frederic blinked. "They're mates?"

"Looks like it. Sage confirmed it, and I believe him."

Frederic's expression softened. "But you and Sage have something, right?"

Reece knew everyone had noticed. That didn't mean he was comfortable with it, or that he was going to confirm that he and Sage had been dancing around each other. "We're friends. That's all."

"You know it's more than that. We all do."

"We're friends," Reece repeated. He needed Frederic to stop pushing. He didn't want to break down in front of his best friend, and that was what would happen if Frederic continued asking questions.

"I see you don't want to talk about that. That's fine."

Reece could have kissed Frederic for finally getting the hint. "You should go back to the party."

Frederic peered at Reece, and Reece held his breath. He needed some time alone. He already knew that the memories would come back, as strong as if everything was happening all over again. He needed to be alone to go through that. When he broke down, he wanted no one to see it, not even his best friend.

"I'm going. I'm going. I'm just worried about you, and so is everyone else," Frederic said. His voice was softer.

Reece suspected Frederic felt sorry for him. Reece hated that, but he couldn't bring himself to care much, not when the memories were already flooding his mind. He always had a hard time ignoring them when this kind of thing happened, and Carey had definitely triggered something. "I'll be fine," he insisted.

"Maybe. Maybe not. I don't think even you know. But I'm here if you need anything, even if it's only to talk. You're my best friend, even though we were away from each other for years. That hasn't changed, and it never will, even though you're so very different since you came back. I'm here for you, whatever you need. And I'm not the only one."

Reece knew that. That was the only reason he was still with the pack. It would have been easier for him to start a new life somewhere else, somewhere no one knew him, but this was good, too. No one in the pack knew about his mate and their daughter. No one in the pack knew Reece had lost both of them. That meant they didn't ask questions, but they were there for Reece when he needed them.

Now wasn't one of those moments. The only thing Reece needed was to be alone, and he was grateful to see Frederic's back as he left.

CHAPTER TWO

When Sage opened his eyes the next morning, he still had no idea what to do. He stared at the ceiling above his bed and thought about the evening before.

He'd met his mate. He'd probably lost Reece and any chance for them to have more than friendship.

Sage sighed and pulled the blankets up until they reached his chin.

He also couldn't stop thinking about what Carey had said—that he didn't mind about Reece being in Sage's life. He'd talked about having more than two people in a relationship, about throuples, and while Sage hoped he'd understood that right, he wasn't sure he had. What if he'd gotten that wrong? What if he'd misinterpreted what Carey had been trying to say?

He couldn't give himself hope that he could have both Carey and Reece in his life. Not yet. He needed to be sure first, and that was only going to happen if he talked to both Carey and Reece.

He was looking forward to neither of those things.

A knock on his front door made him wonder who was already hounding him, and he decided to stay in bed. Whoever it was would leave eventually.

Sage was sure it was Sam as soon as he heard the front door open. Sam was the only one who came and went in the house as much as he wanted to, because he'd lived with Sage for a while before moving in with Frederic. Toby was another possibility, since he and Sage were also friends, but not as close,

15

and Toby was always more reserved. He wouldn't come in like this, not when he knew something had happened to Sage last night. So it had to be Sam, and while Sage loved his best friend, he wasn't looking forward to talking to him, not about this.

"Sage? Are you still in bed?"

Yep, Sam. Sage groaned loud enough for Sam to hear him downstairs.

Sam chuckled. "All right. Stay where you are. I'll bring some coffee and breakfast upstairs."

"I love you," Sage yelled.

"Don't let Frederic hear you."

But Sage did love Sam—as a friend, of course. He'd never had this. He'd never had someone who knew him well enough to understand that he was hiding and trying not to think, someone who knew he needed coffee before talking about what had happened. Even before he'd come to the pack, he'd been a loner. He still was, even though he was surrounded by people. Sam was different. He was special. He was the only best friend Sage had ever had, and Sage didn't want to lose him.

He listened to Sam moving around downstairs and smiled. Anyone would smile when Sam took care of them, and that included Sage. He was used to having Sam around, even though Sam had moved in with his mate.

He heard the footsteps and sat up in bed, making sure to keep the blankets around his waist. He wanted to be able to burrow under them again as soon as he could.

Sam stepped in, holding a tray and smiling. "I'm not surprised."

"I should probably have come downstairs for breakfast."

"Why should you? You deserve to be spoiled, and this is nothing." Sam put the tray on Sage's thighs. "Dig in. Then we'll talk."

Sage wasn't looking forward to that, but he knew Sam could help him make sense of everything that had happened, so he focused on his food, eating as fast as he could while Sam sipped on his own cup of coffee.

Sam waited until Sage was done eating. "Everyone saw you with Carey last night."

Sage leaned back against the headboard. "You know him."

"Toby told me about him. You know he and his brother are living with Toby and Camden right now?"

"Right." Sage had forgotten that. He was pretty sure he'd forgotten a lot of things in his confusion. "What's he like?"

"Honestly? I'm not sure. Toby said he's a good guy. Talks a lot. Loves a little coffee with his sugar. That's about it, though. I've never talked to him."

Sage sighed and rubbed his face. "He's my mate."

There was a pause, and Sage could feel Sam's gaze on him. He didn't want to look at him. Sam wouldn't push, but Sage knew he needed to talk with someone, and Sam was the perfect person for that.

"How does that make you feel?" Sam asked.

Sage snorted and took a sip of coffee. "How do you think it makes me feel? I'm in love with Reece. I've been waiting for him to realize that for years. I *yearned* for something more than friendship with him for just as long. And now everything is ruined."

Sam put his empty mug of coffee on the nightstand and sat cross-legged on the bed, having kicked off his shoes. "Are you sure about that? Because even though Carey is your mate, you don't have to be with him."

"I don't know. I don't know anything right now, Sam. I know I don't have to be with Carey, but can I give up this chance to be with my mate? And what about Reece? I've been giving him hints, yet he's still only a friend. I know he loves me, too. There has to be a reason he doesn't want to be with me."

"He's in love with you?" Sam asked, his voice quieter.

Sage nodded. "I don't know why he's never tried anything else."

"You could ask him."

Sage shook his head. "I can't. I can feel his love for me, but I can also feel how sad it makes him. I don't want him to have to face it."

Sam knew Sage was an empath, so Sage didn't have to explain how his gift worked. Sam understood. He was a unicorn shifter, and while their gifts weren't the same, they were also similar. The gifts were something most shifters didn't have. They were specific to their kind of shifter, and sometimes, Sage wished he could be just a rabbit shifter. Instead, he was a jackalope, and he could feel other people's emotions.

Sam tapped his fingertips onto his knee. "Okay. Let's think about this. You're in love with Reece. You know Reece is in love with you, but you can also feel that something is blocking him. Probably something in his past."

"You can't know that."

"Not for sure. But I know Reece was away for college and then work for almost fifteen years. And he came back about seven years ago, if I'm not wrong. He never talks about what happened during those years, and even Camden thinks it's weird and that he wasn't the same guy when he came back. He was withdrawn, as if something happened to him while he was away."

Sage frowned. "But he's been back for years. Surely he would have talked to someone." But if he hadn't told Frederic, chances were that he hadn't. Of course, Sam might not know whether Reece had talked to Frederic.

"Not as far as I know."

"Okay. It *is* weird. And maybe it has something to do with how he's been behaving with me. That doesn't change anything, though. He still doesn't want anything with me, even though he loves me. Then there's Carey to consider."

"Well, again, you don't *have* to be with him if you don't feel like it."

"But I also don't want to take the possibility of having his mate away from him. It wouldn't be fair."

"Maybe not, but you have to think of yourself first. Look, I'm sure Carey is a great guy. He sure seems like it. But you can't think of him before you think of yourself. You're the most important thing here. You. Not him, not Reece. I know you're not used to thinking of yourself that way, but it's the truth. I'm not saying you have to kick Carey's ass to the curb or to tell Reece anything, or even to date Carey. You don't have to do anything you don't want. But you need to think hard about this. It's *your* future that's in the balance here, and once you make a decision, you won't be able to change your mind without hurting people and yourself."

That was what Sage was afraid of. He didn't know what to do. He didn't know how to make that decision.

But he had to.

Carey checked his reflection in the mirror one last time. When he turned around to leave the bathroom, he saw his brother staring at him from the open door and jerked back. "What the fuck are you doing? You're a creep."

He pushed past Lennox, but of course, Lennox followed him into the bedroom. Carey huffed. He knew he couldn't avoid this conversation, no matter how much he wanted to. He might as well face it right now.

He turned and looked at Lennox, crossing his arms over his chest. "Okay. Let's hear it."

Lennox shook his head. "I don't know what you're talking about."

"Of course you do. There's a reason you're following me around. I want to hear it now before I leave. I have things to do." As it was, he was planning to speak to Sage or Reece, or possibly both of them. It would depend on who he found when he went looking as soon as Lennox was done.

Lennox looked him up and down. "You're going out."

Carey rolled his eyes. "How did you guess? Is it because I made myself pretty?"

Lennox merely stared at Carey.

Carey sighed. He knew his brother cared about him. Carey should probably try to stop being snarky for a minute and listen to what Lennox had to say.

"I'm just worried," Lennox finally said.

"You have nothing to be worried about."

"Are you sure about that? Because as far as I know, your mate has a boyfriend."

Carey grinned. "I know. Isn't it great?"

Lennox shook his head. "I don't understand. Sage is your mate. How can you be happy that he already has someone in his life? How can you be happy that Reece has probably already been in his bed?"

Carey wasn't surprised Lennox didn't understand him. No one did. Lennox might be his brother, and he would always be there for him, but that didn't mean he shared Carey's opinion. "I get what you're saying, but to me, it doesn't matter."

"But how?"

Carey might have been offended if anyone else had asked him that question. It was incredibly private. But Lennox was his twin brother. They'd always been together, ever since they'd been conceived. Carey knew that would change now, and in a way, he didn't want it to. He was also more than ready to start a life with Sage and Reece, though. He and Lennox were going to have to put some distance between them, and he wasn't looking forward to it. He knew Lennox wasn't, either, and that was part of why he was worried. "The way I see it, if the three of us can make it work, it will be twice the love." Carey's smile widened. "And twice the sex. Ever think about that?"

Lennox chuckled. "Trust you to think with your little head. Yes, I *have* thought about that, and you know how much experience I have with having two people in my bed. That's not what I was talking about. Sex in three can be fun, sure. But what about love? What about your life in a relationship? It's not the same, Carey. You can't act as if it is."

"Why not? I already know it's not going to be easy." Mostly because he could tell Reece would have a problem with it. Whatever was going on between Sage and Reece had been underway for a long time. It would be hard for Carey to slip his way into that, but he was resilient and stubborn. "It's going to be so worth it, though."

"I just don't get it. Aren't you jealous?"

That was always the question, wasn't it? "You know I'm not a jealous person."

Lennox snorted. "Understatement of the year, but yeah. Sage is your mate, though. It's not the same thing."

Carey sighed and sat on the edge of the mattress. He wanted to go out, but Lennox was as important to him as Sage and Reece were. Carey needed to take the time to make sure his brother was okay. Lennox had always been such a huge part of his life, and that wasn't going to change, no matter how many men Carey had in his life. "I know you and a lot of people don't understand. I don't care about that."

"Again, not surprised. I'm just worried."

Carey wasn't sure how to explain. He'd already tried, and Lennox didn't seem to be able to understand. "Look. Love grows. It's not a finite emotion, which means that I can love two people at the same time."

"I know that. I keep getting stuck on the fact that Sage is

your mate. The two of you share a bond you can't share with Reece."

"And why should that matter? Why should my relationship with Reece or Sage be different? The bond is just a bond. It doesn't bring anything special. It's just a sign from the universe that this guy might be the perfect guy for me. It doesn't force me to do anything. It's just, I don't know, a hint. I can take it or leave it." And Carey had every intention of taking it, and Reece at the same time. "I already know I can be in love with two people, and I don't see why I should be jealous of what Sage and Reece have. As long as they're happy, I'm happy. I already know they share something I don't have a place in, just like each of them will share something with me the other won't have a place in. Makes sense?"

Lennox shook his head. "Not really, but I wasn't trying to tell you this was wrong. I never would. It's your life, your mate, and you're the one making decisions. I hope you won't regret it, and that you won't get hurt."

Carey rose from the bed and clapped his brother's shoulder. "I already know I'll get hurt. That's what happens when you're in a relationship, especially with two guys."

"You know what I mean. I'm not talking about getting hurt because of the relationship and stuff that's normal and that everyone experiences. I'm talking about you getting hurt because Sage or Reece, or both of them, might eventually want out of the relationship, and you'll be alone."

That thought was terrifying. Carey didn't think he'd be able to stay with the pack if that happened, but that wouldn't make him stop. He was going to take this chance. "How about when people break up? Isn't that the same thing?"

"I guess."

"It is. Yes, there's a possibility that neither Sage nor Reece will want to be with me. There's a possibility they might want to try but find out it's not something they can do. There's also the possibility one of them will want a relationship with me and not with the other." Although Carey had to admit that probably wouldn't happen. Reece and Sage were already in love with each other. Right now, he was the outsider.

He didn't mind. He'd been the outsider all his life, and he knew how to play with that. Discovering Sage was giving him a chance to finally have a family and find his place in life. He'd never thought he'd have that. People were usually afraid of phoenix shifters, and Carey knew they had a reputation among other shifters. It was probably well earned, especially considering his own personality, but he didn't care about that, either. What he *did* care about was that he and Lennox might have finally found a place to call home, and he would never do anything to mess that up, for himself, but more importantly, for his brother.

He smiled at Lennox. "I know you're worried. But you can stop playing big brother. You're only a few minutes older than me, after all."

Lennox glared. "I hope you know what you're doing, Carey. But you know I'm always here if you need to talk."

"You mean, you're always here to listen." Lennox didn't usually say a lot. Actually, Carey was surprised at how much Lennox had said just now. It wasn't like him. "I know you worry. I get it. But I think we've finally found a place to settle down, and I'm not going to mess that up. I want Sage and Reece both. I'll do everything I can to make our relationship work. I promise." And Carey always kept his promises.

Reece didn't have the energy to get up this morning. He hadn't slept well, and he was using staying in bed as an excuse. Maybe he'd fall asleep again.

Or maybe not. He doubted that would happen, considering he kept thinking about Sage and Carey together.

23

He huffed and rolled onto his stomach, burying his face against his pillow. He couldn't help but wonder what had happened between Sage and Carey yesterday after he'd left the party. He desperately wanted to know, but he knew better than to call Sage and ask.

It wasn't his business. It had never been, and it never would be. Sage and Carey were mates, and what they did didn't matter. They shared a bond Reece couldn't compete with — even if he'd been able to get over his past and the memories.

He'd had a terrible night. He hadn't been able to stop thinking about Emily and Sarah. Just that morning, his throat had felt tight and his heart had felt like it was about to explode in his chest. He always felt this way when he thought about his mate and their daughter. He hadn't even gotten to hold Sarah for long, but he would never forget that emotion, that feeling of a family being complete.

Then he'd lost them both. He'd already been losing them when he'd held Sarah to his chest, and he hadn't even known it. She'd been so small, and he knew the doctors had thought they were doing a good thing by handing him his dying daughter. Maybe they were. But now he had to live with the memories and the what-ifs, and he wasn't sure he could, not anymore.

Sage had been a nice distraction. Reece had let himself hope that maybe he could be normal again, that he could have a life that wasn't loneliness and memories. He knew better. He *should* have known better, and now the reality had slapped him in the face, and here he was.

Had Sage and Carey gone home together last night? Probably. It wouldn't be like Sage, but from what Reece knew about Carey, it would be exactly like *him* to do something like that. Besides, Carey was Sage's mate. No one would blame Sage if he had sex with the guy on the first day they met. Most people did when they met their mates.

Reece and Emily had. When they'd met in college and had realized they were mates, they'd become one. They hadn't left each other's side until Emily died.

And here Reece was, making himself depressed again. He'd gotten enough of that during the night, and he needed to stop. It was always hard when the memories came back. He usually managed not to think too much about the past, but once he did, he didn't seem to be able to stop, even though he wanted to. He'd always love his mate and daughter. Nothing would change that. *No one* would. But he was still alive, and they weren't. He didn't know why, but that wouldn't change, either. The best thing for him would be to try to ignore his past and focus on his future, no matter how bleak it was.

But when he tried to stop thinking about Emily and Sarah, his thoughts went to Sage and Carey, and he wasn't sure which was worse. Neither was healthy for him, that was for sure. He should probably get up and do something — putter around the house — try to convince himself that nothing had happened and that his life was just the way it had been yesterday.

So he did.

He finally got out of bed, showered, and tried to put yesterday behind him. He already knew it would be hard, but he'd made his decision when it came to Sage a long time ago. He'd lost his mate. He couldn't go through it again.

Of course, Sage *wasn't* his mate. He was Carey's. That didn't mean that Reece wasn't in love with him, though. He was, and the thought of losing him was terrifying. Reece had kept himself back because he hadn't wanted to go through that. Staying away hadn't changed anything in the end. Reece was still hurting over losing Sage.

His plan had backfired spectacularly.

Reece should have known better — and he should have

acted differently. He should have left the pack. He probably shouldn't have come back in the first place, but after roaming the country doing odd jobs in the hope that eventually the pain of losing his mate would fade, he'd given up. He needed a home. He needed his family, his friends, and that was why he had come back. Sage had been a nice distraction, but Reece had always known nothing would happen with him. He couldn't allow it to.

He wanted Sage to be happy, and he wasn't the man who could make that happen. He didn't know if Carey was, but the fact that he and Sage were mates pointed that way. Reece hoped Sage would get everything he hadn't had with Emily. Sage deserved it. No one knew his story except for Camden, but Reece knew there was pain in Sage's past. Hopefully, Carey would be the man who would help him get past that and heal. Reece hadn't been able to. He hadn't tried to.

And now he'd never be able to.

A knock on the front door made Reece look up from the dishes he was washing. He wasn't surprised that Frederic was already back, checking in on him. His best friend had been worried since Reece had come back to the pack seven years ago, and while he'd stop asking questions, Reece knew they were always there, just waiting to pop out of his mouth. Eventually, Reece would talk to Frederic about Emily and Sarah again, but not now. He hadn't in the past seven years, and he still wasn't anywhere near ready to.

But leaving Frederic on the doorstep wasn't going to work. He would continue to knock until Reece opened, so Reece turned the water off, grabbed a towel, and dried his hands as he walked to the front door. He swung it open, a small, indulgent smile already on his lips when he froze.

It wasn't Frederic knocking on his door. It was Sage, and he'd never looked so good.

He looked hesitant but gorgeous. There was a light in him

that Reece had never seen, and he couldn't help but wonder if meeting Carey had already changed him.

Reece cleared his throat, forcing himself to stop thinking about that. "Sage. What are you doing here?"

Sage raised a hand and glared at him. "Shut up."

Reece snapped his mouth shut, his eyes growing round. Had Sage just told him to shut up? That wasn't like him. Reece wanted to ask what was happening, but he knew. That was Carey's influence already, and no matter how much Reece hated it, he knew it was a good thing. It was time for Sage to speak up for himself, to stop hiding, no matter what he was hiding from.

Sage nodded when he realized that Reece was listening. "Good. I need you to shut up while I speak, okay? This is already hard enough as it is without being interrupted, and I need to be able to say everything I have to say before you speak. Okay?"

Reece arched a brow. Sage didn't want him to speak, and he wasn't going to.

Sage rolled his eyes. "You can nod if you understood."

Reece nodded. He was curious to see where this was going. He had about a thousand questions about Sage and Carey, but he hadn't been about to ask them anyway. This was better. It gave him a little time with Sage before he went back to his mate. He didn't care what this was about.

Sage sucked in a breath. "Okay. I have something to tell you." He looked down, then up at Reece again. He raked a hand through his hair.

Reece's chest squeezed. Sage was nervous, and he couldn't begin to imagine why.

"All right. I can do this." Sage looked Reece straight in the eyes. "I love you. I'm in love with you. I have been for a while, and I should've told you right away instead of dancing around it. And before you say anything, I don't care about the mate thing. I want *you*. I know Carey and I are mates, but that doesn't mean we have to be together. I don't want to be with him if I can't have you. You're the man I love, not him. If having you means I'm going to lose him, then I'm ready for that to happen."

Reece knew his eyes were wide, and he opened his mouth to answer, but what was he supposed to say to that? He'd never thought this moment would happen, even though he'd imagined it often. Sage loved him, and he loved Sage. What was next for them, though?

He already knew, and even though he didn't like it, it was time to be honest with Sage.

CHAPTER THREE

Sage couldn't breathe. He waited for Reece to answer, to say something, *anything*, but Reece just stared at him. His eyes were wide and his mouth was slightly open, and Sage started to worry.

Was Reece in shock? Surely he had to have realized that Sage had feelings for him before now. Sage thought he had, but maybe not. Maybe he really was surprised. Sage wanted to push, to ask him if he'd heard him, to demand an answer, but he knew better.

So he waited. He waited and held his breath, praying that he would hear the answer he wanted. He also prayed that he hadn't just made a mistake, possibly the biggest of his entire life.

He expected Reece to reject him. Even though Reece loved him, he also was aware that something had happened to Reece, had given him a reason to avoid Sage. Sage didn't know what that something was, and he doubted he'd get answers if he asked. But he knew it was important, and he knew it would probably continue to keep Reece and him apart.

He needed to try, though. He would never forgive himself if he gave up on Reece without doing everything he could. Now Reece knew that Sage was in love with him, and the ball was in his court. He was the one who had to make the play.

Reece finally unfroze and rubbed his face

Suddenly, Sage realize how tired he looked. Maybe blurting out all of that hadn't been the best idea. Sage hadn't allowed himself to think about it too much. He knew he'd chicken out if he did, and this had to be done.

Reece stepped aside. "Why don't you come in?"

That was much more than Sage had expected. He'd thought that Reece would reject him, tell him he didn't feel the same way. Sage would have known it was a lie, but Reece didn't know he was an empath. No one did except Camden and Sam, and no one had looked into it, as far as Sage knew. It would be fairly easy for them to find out, since that was a power that was associated with jackalope shifters, but again, not a lot of people knew what kind of shifter he was. He carefully avoided shifting along with the rest of the pack. He had to.

He walked into Reece's house and looked around. He didn't think he'd ever been inside, and he was curious. If this was the only time he visited, he wanted to see as much as he could.

The place looked warm and comfortable, with soft colors on the wall and several framed pictures up. There was a carpet at the bottom of the stairs, and shoes were piled on a rack. Coats hung by the door, and everywhere, it smelled like Reece.

Reece closed the door behind Sage, and together they stood in the entrance, staring at each other. Sage waited for Reece to say something, and he steeled himself against the rejection.

That wasn't what came, though.

"I love you too," Reece murmured.

Sage's heart felt like it froze in his chest for a second. He sucked in a breath, then another, and struggled to make sense of what he'd just heard.

"But things can't work between us," Reece continued.

Sage blinked and allowed the words to sink in. "Why not?" Reece didn't owe him an explanation, but Sage hoped he would get one.

"There's a reason I didn't tell you about this until now,"

Reece said. "I wanted to. I've been in love with you for you what feels like years. But we can't."

Sage shook his head. "Whatever it is, I don't care."

Reece opened his mouth, but a knock on the door interrupted whatever he was about to say. Sage almost stomped his feet in frustration, but he could see the relief in Reece's expression when he reached for the front door. He was grateful someone had interrupted them, at least for a second.

Then he opened the door, and Carey was standing there, grinning at them.

Reece shut down. There was no other way to describe it. His expression shuttered, and he looked once again cold and careless. "What do you want?" he asked, and even his voice was different. It was harsher, and it was obvious he didn't care for Carey.

That didn't seem to deter Carey, though. "I just saw Sage walk in, and I thought I'd come by."

"You're right. He's here. And since we're done talking, I'm sure he won't have a problem going with you."

Carey shook his head and stepped into the house, pushing Reece inside without touching him. Reece's eyes widened, and he took a step back to avoid Carey touching him, and by the time Sage realized what was happening, Carey was inside and the front door was closed again.

"What do you think you're doing?" Reece snarled.

"I thought that was obvious. Are the two of you talking about your relationship?"

"It's none of your business."

"Of course it is. Sage is my mate, and you're his boyfriend. That makes both of you my boyfriends, right?"

Reece blinked.

Sage had already heard that theory, so he wasn't surprised, but he had a hard time believing Carey meant it. Was it really that easy? Not that it would be, of course, but it was a chance

Sage hadn't thought he'd have.

He wanted Reece in his life. That much he was sure of. He also didn't want to lose the chance to be with his mate, though. The two things shouldn't go together, yet from what Carey was saying, they just might, and Sage found himself holding his breath as he waited for Reece to answer.

"What are you talking about?" Reece asked.

Carey's gaze moved from Reece to Sage. "What were the two of you talking about?" he asked instead of answering.

"I told him I'm in love with him," Sage said since he was pretty sure that Reece wouldn't be honest, not with Carey, not about this.

Reece groaned. "Why did you tell Carey that? He's your mate. You shouldn't go around telling other men you're in love with me, and you especially shouldn't tell Carey about it."

Sage glared at him and crossed his arms over his chest. "Even if it's true?"

Reece shook his head.

He looked defeated, and Sage didn't like it.

"You don't understand, Sage."

"You're right. I don't. I want to, though. I told you I didn't care about whatever the reason is that you don't want to be with me."

"It's not that I don't want to be with you. I do. More than anything in the world right now. But I can't allow myself to fall in love with you."

Carey snorted softly. "From what you just said, it's a bit late for that."

Reece glared at him. "I should kick you out."

"Maybe. Are you going to, though?"

Sage knew the answer even before Reece shook his head. Whatever was happening, Reece was confused, and probably curious. Sage knew *he* was. He wanted to listen to what Carey had to say. He wanted to find out if the three of them could have this, whatever *this* was.

This wasn't what he'd imagined his life would be like. When he'd run, he'd thought he would have to be alone for the rest of his life. Most people, most packs, would use him if they found out what he could do. They wouldn't be safe. But not Camden. Not the Rosewood pack. Here, Sage had been given a safe place to stay, a place that had become home. He'd made friends, albeit only a few. He'd fallen in love, and he was loved in return.

And he'd met his mate.

He was at the cusp of something important, something that would change the rest of his life. He had no idea how the balance would tilt, though.

Carey might as well go straight to the point. That way, he would avoid misunderstandings. It was the best thing, because he didn't want Sage and Reece to freak out. He could tell they were shocked. He'd probably better explain what he meant.

He cleared his throat. "I know you're in love with Sage, and that Sage is in love with you. I know that at least in the beginning, I'll be the one looking in from the outside. And that's okay. The bond me and Sage share doesn't mean we have to be together, but I'd like to be with him, and I realized that along with him, you come too, Reece."

Reece shook his head. "Sage and I aren't together."

"I know. I have no idea why, but I suspect you have a good reason, or maybe that you *think* you have a good reason." He turned his attention to Sage. "And of course, both of you can say no. I don't expect anything from this relationship, or even a relationship at all. Like I said, the bond we share doesn't mean we have to be together." But Carey hoped they would because he wanted this. He wanted Sage and Reece and a home. "I'll understand if the answer is no and if neither of you wants anything to do with me. But if you're both okay with it, I'd like to get to know both of you with the intent of being in a throuple."

Reece made a strangled sound. "A throuple?"

"You know. When three people are together in a relationship."

Reece glared — which seemed to be something he often did in Carey's experience. "I know what a throuple is. I'm not stupid."

"So what's the problem?"

"You can't want to be with both of us."

"Why not?" Carey understood it wasn't conventional, and he wasn't surprised to find that Reece's first instinct was to say no, but he hoped that after taking some time to think about it, Reece would be more amenable.

"What does that involve?" Sage asked. He didn't seem to be as against it as Reece.

Carey turned his attention back to him. "Just what you'd expect from a relationship between two people. I want to date and to get to know both of you. I'd like to eventually fall in love with both of you and have the two of you fall in love with me. I know this isn't conventional. I know it's going to be hard. But I have experience in this, albeit none of them with my mate. I think we can do it, as long as we all agree, of course, and as long as we talk. That's going to be the most important part of this. We'll need to talk even more than people in normal two-person relationships do."

Sage bit his lower lip. "But you think we can do this? That we can be a throuple, like you said?"

"I hope so. I don't want to give up on what we have. The bond might not mean we have to be together, but it's there for a reason, and I don't want to ignore it. I also can't ignore the fact that you and Reece are in love, though. I don't want to break the two of you apart. If that means that I have to welcome Reece in our relationship, then I'm fine with that." He looked at Reece up and down. "More than fine." He wiggled his eyebrows, and while he wasn't surprised to see Reece glare, he was happy for the smile that finally bloomed on Sage's lips.

"And you think it can work?" Sage asked.

Carey could hear hope in his voice, and he shared it. He knew that Reece was going to be the hard spot in this, though. Whatever his reason for keeping Sage at arm's length, the same would go for Carey. Carey and Sage would find a way in eventually, but that would only happen if Reece gave them the opportunity to do that. If he didn't, if he closed himself off, then the future Carey had imagined would be gone. He wasn't sure he'd lose Sage, but he hoped he wouldn't. If he couldn't have both men, he at least wanted his mate.

But ideally, he *really* wanted both of them in his life.

He raked a hand through his hair, only to remember how much care he'd put into making sure he looked good. "I just want a chance, okay? That's all I'm saying. I know this isn't going to be easy. That's fine with me. This will be worth putting work into it. I'm ready to do that."

"But you don't live here," Sage pointed out.

"I will if the two of you want me. My brother and I have been looking for a home for so long. I hope I've finally found it with the two of you."

This was going to be the hardest thing Carey would ever do, wasn't it? And not because of Sage. If it was just him, Carey was pretty sure they'd be closer to dating already. But there was Reece to consider, and while he did make the situation more complicated, Carey wasn't lying when he said that it would be worth trying even more.

Sage wasn't going anywhere without Reece. Sage seemed

to be on board with the throuple thing, but whatever had held Reece back from a relationship with him would keep him back from a relationship with Carey, too. Carey would have to find a way around that.

He wasn't sure he could. Sage hadn't managed, and Reece was in love with him. So far, the only thing Sage felt for Carey was probably annoyance and maybe wanting to kick him out of his house.

But Carey could deal with that. He'd dealt with worse, and he'd come out the winner. This wouldn't be any different. Reece wouldn't know what hit him. Carey was stubborn, and he never gave up, even when most people would have.

He was going to find a way to get under Reece's skin. He was going to make both Sage and Reece fall in love with him, and he was going to make both of them blissfully happy. Once they were, they wouldn't be able to imagine a life without him.

And he would have found his home—a home for him and Lennox.

He just had to find a way around Reece. He needed Reece to open up to him, at least a bit, enough for him to take a step in.

He had no idea where to start, though. He didn't know Reece well enough. But Sage did, and hard work had never frightened Carey. Together, he knew they could do this. Together, they could convince Reece that the three of them should be together, that they would be happy if he allowed that to happen.

It was time to start this battle, and Carey was more than ready to fight it.

Reece had thought he was shocked when Sage told him he loved him. But what was he supposed to say to *this*?

No. He wanted to say no. He even opened his mouth to tell Carey that, but he couldn't get the word past his lips. He closed them again, sucked in a breath, and thought.

He wanted to hope he wasn't about to lose Sage. He wanted to imagine how this could work, and he wondered if it could, if he would be able to share Sage.

He didn't know. He wanted Sage for himself, but he'd never allowed himself to have him, and for good reasons. He also didn't want to take away the possibility of Sage being with his mate. That would be too cruel, just like it was in his case. Emily had died, and Reece would never get her back. Sage could be with Carey, though. He deserved to be. And even Carey, who Reece found annoying and rude, deserved to be with Sage. Besides, Reece knew the only reason he didn't like Carey was because of Sage. He probably would have become a friend if Sage hadn't been in the picture.

Reece wanted to kick the two of them out. He wanted to protect his heart, which was already bruised and battered. It would be the best thing to do. He *needed* to protect himself.

But he couldn't help but ask, "Do you really just want to start with a date?"

Carey blinked as if he hadn't expected Reece to say yes. And Reece wasn't, not yet. Maybe not ever. "Sure. We can start dating." His smile widened. Was the guy always smiling? "Is that something you might want?"

Reece shook his head. "I don't know."

His last date had been with Emily. Was everything going to remind him of her for the rest of his life? Probably. But he couldn't deny that the memories, the feeling that his life was all wrong and missing a vital part, had faded over the years. He would always love Emily, and of course, Sarah. They would always be part of his life. He wouldn't have it any other way.

But they were dead. They had died more than fourteen

years ago. It had been the hardest thing Reece had ever gone through, but he'd survived. He was still alive, although some days, he wondered if he actually was and if there was any point to it.

He'd forced himself to be dead inside since their deaths. It had been easier to deal with. He didn't have to face the pain, even though it had seeped into his every cell. But now there was Sage to think about, and it looked like Carey was in, too.

Was this something Reece could do? Could he date both Sage and Carey and see where this would go?

But if he agreed, what would happen? Obviously, Carey had asked him out because he wanted things to work between the three of them. That meant that if things went the way he wanted, he and Sage were going to be part of Reece's life for a long time. They were going to be together. Eventually, they would move in together, settle in his life the way Reece would have done with Emily if he could have. The thought of having that was terrifying. Reece wasn't sure he could deal with it. He'd never tried after losing Emily, and now that he had a chance at it, his first instinct was to say no and take a step back.

He didn't want to, though.

He'd kept himself away from Sage because he thought it was the best thing for both of them. He still did. He still was afraid of hurting, of repeating what he'd already gone through. He wouldn't survive that — he was sure of it. No one survived that kind of loss twice.

But could he close himself off from life? Because that was what he'd been doing. It had been easy to focus on his work, on Frederic, on the house.

Except at night. When he was alone in bed, he yearned for someone in his arms, for someone's breath on his skin. The loneliness was a deep ache in his chest, an ache he hadn't been able to heal.

Because he hadn't allowed himself to.

He knew he could have had that with Sage a long time ago. The only reason he didn't was because of himself. He still wasn't sure he could do this, but his thoughts were tilting toward saying yes, and he didn't understand why.

He'd worked so hard to keep Sage away. He'd worked to make himself lonely because it had been the safest option for his heart. And now he didn't want to be anymore. He wanted someone to hug him. He wanted someone to share the burdens of life. And if he said yes, he would have *two* someones. It wasn't something he'd ever thought he'd have. Even in his wildest dreams, his future had been centered around Sage, and only him. But now there was Carey to think about.

What did Carey want? Could he possibly want both Sage and Reece? That was what he'd said, and Reece knew he'd heard him right. He couldn't help but wonder if that was the truth, though. "You want me because Sage is in love with me," he said.

Carey cocked his head as if trying to understand what Reece was saying. "Of course. I know the two of you are a package deal. I want to take that deal."

Reece couldn't help but smile. Did anything bring Carey down, ever? "That's not what I meant."

Carey nodded. "You're asking if I would have looked at you twice if I'd met you in the street instead of you being associated with Sage."

Reece was embarrassed, but he nodded. He wanted to be sure if Carey was doing this because he wanted to or because he thought he had to.

Carey's smile widened even more, something Reece hadn't thought possible. "Hell, yes. Have you looked at yourself in the mirror lately? Because you're hot. And let's be honest, right now, that's the only thing I like about you and Sage both. I don't know you. I just know that Sage is my mate, that he's

39

in love with you, and that both of you are gorgeous. But that's going to change. That's why I want to date. I want to get to know the two of you, and the sooner that happens, the sooner I'll fall in love with you, too."

Reece barked out a laugh. He couldn't help it. "You're so convinced we're going to fall in love."

Carey took a step closer, and Reece had to force himself to stay where he was. He was used to keeping people at arm's length, and it felt weird to allow someone in his personal space. Carey leaned closer, *closer*, and kissed Reece's cheek. "I know we're going to fall in love. I'm sure of that," he murmured.

Then he was gone, and for whatever reason, Reece wanted him back.

It was ridiculous. He'd never been in a threesome. Hell, he hadn't had sex in the past fourteen or so years. The last person he'd been with was Emily. He'd thought about it, of course. But he'd never been this tempted. The only one who had tempted him as much was Sage, and he was right there, with his eyes wide and full of hope.

Sage seemed to want this. He wanted it as much as Carey did, even if Reece didn't understand why. For whatever reason, he'd fallen in love with Reece, and he wanted them to be together.

Could Reece continue to push him away? Especially with Carey in the mix now. Even if Reece said no, he suspected Carey would push. That seemed to be his style.

He didn't want to be hounded. He didn't want to run, either, not anymore. He was tired, and he wanted more to life than what he'd had until now — than what he'd *forced* himself to have until now.

And he could have more. He just had to say yes.

So he did. "All right."

Carey's eyes widened. "Yes? We're going on a date? The

three of us?"

Reece nodded. He hoped he wouldn't regret it, but even if he did, Sage's smile was worth it. "I'm coming on a date with both of you." And he prayed everything would go the right way, although he wasn't yet sure what the right way was.

CHAPTER FOUR

This was it. It was the day Sage went on a date with Reece — and to everyone's surprise, Carey.

Sage had a hard time believing this was happening. He'd been thinking about it since Carey had barged into his and Reece's life a few days ago. Carey had managed to obtain what Sage hadn't in so many years. He'd convinced Reece to give them a chance.

Both of them.

Sage wasn't sure what to think of that, and right now, he didn't *want* to think about it. He couldn't help but feel hopeful. He was going on a date with Reece, something he'd wanted for almost as long as he'd known Reece. He didn't know if Carey had other gifts beyond creating and controlling fire, but he sure seemed to be able to convince people to do what he wanted. Not that Sage was sad about that. He was getting Reece, and he'd been ready to do just about anything for that to happen. Where Carey had worn Reece down after only a conversation, Sage had been trying for years.

He didn't know what had changed, but he didn't think it mattered. He, Reece, and Carey were going on a date in an hour or so, and he never been so happy — or so nervous.

He checked his reflection again. He still had time before he needed to head out, but he wanted to look perfect. He wanted Carey to be happy, and he didn't want Reece to regret agreeing to this. He wasn't sure that whatever he wore would make a difference, but he would do everything he could to make the date a good one. It was the only thing he *could* do.

A knock on the door made him huff. It was probably Sam, who knew that Sage was going on a date with both his mate and his boyfriend. Well, not boyfriend yet, but hopefully — by the end of the evening — that was what the three of them would be. Sage didn't like to think differently about Carey and Reece. He wanted both of them to be equal in his eyes, but he realized it would take time. He and Reece had been dancing around each other for a long time, while Carey was new and Sage's mate. He was there, and hopefully, he was there to stay. Eventually, Sage would feel about him the same way he felt about Reece, and the mate bond wouldn't matter to either of them.

A second knock made him swear. He abandoned the mirror and headed downstairs. He was ready to gripe at Sam for disturbing him at this most important time, but when he opened the door, it wasn't Sam.

It was Reece.

Sage looked around, expecting to see Carey, but Carey wasn't there. "Reece?" He could hear his voice trembling, and while he didn't like it, he knew it was a reflection of how he felt.

Was Reece here because he'd change his mind? Was he about to tell Sage that?

Reece rubbed the back of his neck. "Hey, Sage." He looked Sage up and down. "You're beautiful."

Sage's chest expanded. "Thank you." He bit his lower lip. He'd always thought that Reece was a gorgeous man, but he never allowed himself to tell him, of course. Now, he could. "You're not so bad yourself."

To Sage's surprise, Reece's cheeks flushed. "Thanks. I'm not as beautiful as you, but I'll take the compliment."

"Not that I don't like having you here, but I thought we were meeting at the restaurant?" It sounded stupid that the three of them take a different car, but Carey wasn't wrong when he said that they all needed a way to go home if they needed to. It was a first date, and it wasn't a conventional one. Neither Sage nor Reece had ever been with two guys, and Sage was pretty sure he would eventually feel overwhelmed. Maybe having his own car and a way to escape would help keep him calm.

"Oh, I know. That's still what the plan is."

"Yet, you're here."

"I need to talk to you." He straightened his shoulders and looked Sage in the eyes, and Sage knew that something important was going on. He wasn't sure he wanted to find out what that was, though. He was terrified that Reece had changed his mind and that he was there to tell Sage about it. That wasn't what Sage wanted to hear, but if he had to, he was grateful Reece had come to his home rather than wait to do it at the restaurant. Sage didn't want to make a scene, but he'd be crushed if he lost Reece, especially now, after he had hoped.

He stepped to the side. "Come in. We can talk before we go."

Reece was hesitant, but he stepped into the entrance. Sage closed the door and led him to the small living room, gesturing at the couch. Reece sat, but Sage didn't. He wasn't sure he could tolerate sitting next to Reece. He was nervous, and it was always better for him to walk the nervousness away rather than hope it would fade.

Reece didn't say anything about it. Instead, he seemed to be looking for the words to tell Sage whatever he had to tell him, hesitating a few times before finally saying, "I want to explain why I never told you that I loved you, and more importantly, why I kept pushing you away."

That got Sage's attention, and he stopped moving. "You don't have to tell me anything." It still stunned him that Reece had said he loved him. It was something he'd never thought he'd hear coming from him. He'd known about it, of course, and he would have to tell Reece and Carey about his gift sooner rather than later. Not now, though. Not yet. Not when Reece was finally ready to talk to him.

"You're right. I don't *have* to tell you anything. But I want to. It's going to be hard, though. Maybe the hardest thing I've done recently. I've only told Frederic, but I still refuse to talk to him about it, and you know how close I am to him. But you deserve to know."

"It's that important?"

Reece nodded, and Sage wondered if Carey should be there, too. He was new in their lives. He didn't know how Reece had been before he'd stepped in. But whatever this was, it was important to Reece, important enough that he'd been carrying the secret for years. Carey would eventually find out. Sage had no doubt about that. But if Reece felt more comfortable talking to him alone this time, then that was what they would do. He would never push Reece or Carey into anything.

He smiled and hoped it was a reassuring gesture. "I'm listening. You can stop anytime, of course, and as I said, you don't have to tell me anything you're not comfortable with. I love you, Reece. That's not going to change, whatever you tell me."

Reece looked at Sage. His eyes glittered with emotions Sage had to do his best not to read. His first instinct was to open himself to Reece's feelings, but he'd worked hard since he'd arrived in Rosewood and had moved in with the pack to avoid doing just that. He wanted to give people their privacy. He had no business digging into their emotions, especially not Reece's. He could shield himself, even though he could feel Reece's feelings battering at his mind. It wouldn't be right, though.

"You know I left the pack to go to college," Reece started.

Sage nodded. He'd had no idea the story would start so long ago, but it made sense. Something powerful had kept Reece away from him for all these years, and he was about to find out what it was. "I know you only came back seven years ago."

"I did. I needed some time alone after what happened." Reece sucked in a breath. "While I was at college, I met my mate. Her name was Emily."

It felt as if Sage had been sucker-punched. He hadn't expected that. As far as he knew, no one was aware that Reece had met his mate. He understood what Reece had gone through now that he'd met Carey — the happiness, the confusion, the wonder. He didn't know what to tell Reece, so he kept his mouth shut.

Reece didn't seem to care. He went on, "We got together right away. We fell in love. I didn't tell anyone about her, just Frederic." The corner of his lips curled into a half-smile. "I wanted to surprise them. Emily and I were almost done with college. We were going to graduate, then come back here. I was going to introduce her to everyone. And when she got pregnant, it felt like the surprise got even bigger. I was going to come back with a *pregnant* mate. Everyone would be shocked, but so happy, as happy as I was with her."

Sage couldn't help it. He sat next to Reece and took one of his hands, linking their fingers together. He knew Reece needed it. He could feel it, no matter how hard he was trying not to. "You were happy with her," he said in a soft voice.

"Happier than I ever thought I could be." Reece sucked in a trembling breath. "Then she died. They both did. Her and Sarah. I lost both of them when Emily went into labor too soon, and I never recovered from it. I spent the following years roaming around the country, doing odd jobs here and there. I couldn't face coming back home without them." He looked at Sage, and his eyes glittered with tears now. "That's why I kept you at arm's length. I can't go through this a second time. I can't lose you the way I lost them. I couldn't even expose myself to the *possibility* of losing you."

At that moment, Sage's heart shattered for Reece.

"You're not even a little bit worried?" Lennox asked.

He and Carey had just watched Reece walk into Sage's house. Carey had no idea why Reece was there, since the three of them were supposed to meet in about an hour at the restaurant they'd chosen for their first date, but it didn't matter. "Why should I be worried?"

"Because it's obvious there's already something between the two of them." Lennox gestured toward the house. "You saw them. They're alone in there right now. They haven't even told you about this. They're going behind your back."

Carey frowned. "Of course not."

Lennox arched a brow and leaned against the wall. They were on Camden's porch, and Carey was taking a breather before he had to leave. Protecting Toby was a full-time job, even with Lennox, and he wanted to relax for the next hour.

He was nervous. He usually wasn't when it came to dating, but this wasn't just a date. This was the beginning of the rest of his life — of the life he would share with Reece and Sage — and he wanted everything to be perfect. He knew that wasn't possible, but he'd do everything he could to make it happen.

That meant he had to trust Reece and Sage. He *did* trust them. "They're not hiding anything from me. You're right. They didn't tell me they were going to see each other before the date. I don't even know if Sage was aware that Reece was going to talk to him. But even if he was, I don't see why that should be a problem."

Lennox shook his head. "I don't understand you."

He never had, even though they were twins. They were too

different. "I'm not worried. I realize that Reece and Sage have a history together, a history I have nothing to do with. I'm not surprised they want to talk before going out. I'm the outsider here, and I'm going to have to work to become part of their relationship. And that's okay with me. I know that the relationship I'll have with Sage and Reece separately will be different from the one they share, but that's okay with me. I don't resent either of them for something they can't help."

Lennox still didn't look convinced, but thankfully, he didn't push the issue. He was right about one thing, though. Carey was curious about what Reece and Sage were talking about. Probably their relationship. Ideally, Reece was explaining why he hadn't told him he loved him before. Carey knew there was something big there, even though he barely knew Reece. That was the only explanation for keeping Sage away when it was obvious that Reece was crazy about him.

He understood that for their throuple to work, Reece would have to come clean to Sage. It wasn't so much that they couldn't have secrets, but whatever secrets they kept needed to be small ones. It was *not* a small secret. It was probably life-changing, and it was good to see that Reece was finally moving on. Whatever had happened in his past, Carey was sorry for him, but he'd always thought that one shouldn't live in the past. Life was the present and future. That was all that mattered.

He knew that not everyone shared his opinion, though. As far as he was concerned, though, he didn't care about either of his men's pasts. He would be touched if they wanted to tell him about it, and he would listen, but whatever they'd done, whatever had happened to them, didn't matter, not beyond what those situations had turned them into. The past had made them the men they were today. Carey was going to make sure that from now on, he was part of their future.

Lennox's phone rang, and Carey frowned. They didn't

have friends, even though they became friendly with people in just about every shifter group they stayed with. But even when they did, those people were friendly with Carey more than they were with Lennox. Lennox was too intimidating and quiet for people to make friends with him easily. That was why it was weird that his phone was the one ringing, although Carey was relieved. He didn't want to talk to anyone but Lennox, Reece, or Sage right now, and he didn't think Reece or Sage were the ones calling.

Lennox took his phone out of his jeans pocket and looked at the screen. He grimaced, and Carey knew he wouldn't be happy with whatever was about to happen.

"It's Douglas," Lennox said.

Carey grimaced. "You should probably answer." Douglas Peterson was the alpha of the nest Lennox and Carey had ended up with after their own had been decimated. Both their parents had died—their father of a heart attack after the nest had been attacked again and again until only their family remained. It had been too much stress for Carey's dad to protect his family, especially when he'd lost everyone else. Then, Carey and Lennox's mother had poisoned herself.

And she'd left Carey and Lennox alone.

Carey had resented her for a long time, but he didn't anymore. He'd always had Lennox. She'd been left alone after their father had died, so he understood. But her death had left Carey and Lennox on their own. And while Carey had been relieved that Douglas had taken them in, he wasn't anymore.

Carey and Lennox had always felt obligated to help Douglas. His nest was a weird one—almost no one was related by blood, but rather, Douglas collected phoenix shifters. He used them, although not without their consent, of course. He sent them around, following the calls and help requests, from shifters who needed them like the Rosewood pack. Phoenix shifters were rare enough that there was a high demand, especially with what their gift was. As long as they sent money back to the nest, Douglas had never pushed anyone to take a particular job or to do something.

But still. He probably wanted to know when Lennox and Carey would be ready to move on, and he wasn't going to like their answer.

"Douglas," Lennox said as he answered.

"Lennox."

Douglas' voice was muffled, so Carey moved even closer to his brother, leaning right next to him against the wall and pressing his ear on the other side of the phone. It was an awkward position, but he needed to know what was happening, and Lennox hated to put his calls on speaker.

"What can I do for you?" Lennox asked.

"I just wanted to know how long you were going to stay in Rosewood."

Lennox looked at Carey, and Carey shook his head. He didn't think it was a good idea to tell Douglas what was happening, not yet. They needed to talk first. They needed to make decisions they'd been avoiding until now.

Because Carey wasn't going anywhere. He would stay in Rosewood with Reece and Carey. He had to tell Camden about that, though. Camden was the pack's alpha, and he would be the one to decide if Carey was welcome or not.

Carey hoped Lennox would stay, too. The two of them had always been together, and while he realized that they were adults and that they could spend some time away from each other, he didn't want to. It had always been him and Lennox against the world. Now, Carey was finding his own family, and he hated the thought of leaving Lennox behind. He truly hoped Lennox could make Rosewood his home, too, but that was something they needed to talk about, and as soon as possible if they wanted to give Douglas the answer he was looking for.

"I'm not sure," Lennox said. "The Springfield pack is still giving the Rosewood pack problems."

Douglas huffed. "You can't even give me a vague idea?"

"I'm sorry. I'll talk to the alpha if you want me to. He wants to be sure that his mate and his mate's brother are safe, though, and I understand it. The Springfield pack envoy was a dick, and he only backed off when he didn't have a choice."

Douglas laughed. "I heard Carey took care of him."

"He did. So far, they haven't tried anything else, but I don't think that will last for long. They want one of the unicorn shifters, and they won't stop for anything for long to get one."

Carey suspected Lennox was right. He didn't like it. He didn't want anyone threatening his new family and his new home, but at the end of the day, he and Lennox were there to do a job. They were supposed to protect Sam and Toby, and that was what they were going to do.

Whatever happened after that, though, was still uncertain. They had to talk, but not tonight.

Tonight, Carey had a date.

Reece waited for Sage to answer him, to say something. He had no idea what was going through Sage's mind. He knew Sage probably felt sorry for him, but that didn't tell him anything else. Anyone would, and Sage was one of the most tender and gentle men that Reece knew. So yes, he was probably feeling sorry for Reece, but that wasn't why Reece had told him.

He wanted Sage to understand. He wanted him to know that he hadn't kept him at arm's length to hurt him. It had been to protect himself, not because he didn't want Sage in his life.

"Oh, Reece. I'm so sorry for everything you lost," Sage murmured.

Reece nodded, unsure whether or not he could get a word out if he tried. He didn't even want to. He was on the very edge of tears. And while he didn't care about crying in front of anyone, least of all Sage, he'd cried so many times over his loss that he was a bit done with it.

He knew that he would cry again. Losing Emily and Sarah had left a hole in his life, a hole the size of a crater. But he hoped that being with Sage, and yes, with Carey, might start the healing.

Reece understood now that by isolating himself, by pushing everyone away, he'd slowed down that healing and let his pain fester. He'd left the wound open without even attempting to heal it. He viewed his pain as a shield, and it had been the wrong thing to do. It hadn't felt like it at the time, but now, he understood.

"It's okay," Sage continued. "I understand why you don't want me, and it's okay."

Reece shook his head. He didn't want Sage to think he didn't want him. Nothing could be further away from the truth. "Don't you see?" he asked, his voice rough. "I've always wanted you. Ever since the first time I met you, I knew I would fall in love with you, and I did. I still want you, that hasn't changed." Reece didn't think it ever would.

Sage was his second chance. Reece was only thirty-seven. He couldn't be alone for the rest of his life, and he didn't want to be, not anymore.

He knew the memories would always be there and that they would grab at him sometimes, pull him down. He would no doubt feel guilty about being with Sage and Carey, and he would never forget Emily and Sarah. He didn't want to, and he didn't think that Carey and Sage would demand that from him. He didn't know Carey, but he did know Sage. He was a good man, and he would cherish the memories right along with Reece. But more importantly, he would be there when they were too much for Reece to stand against. He would be there to support Reece and help him through it.

Reece raked a hand through his hair. "I'll be honest. I don't know if this can work. I want us to try, though. I'm done pushing you away. I'm done hurting myself and you because I'm afraid of the pain." There would always be pain. The pain of losing Emily and Sarah would always be there, but Reece didn't have to let it suffocate him. He didn't have to be alone.

Sage smiled. "I'm glad you think that way. Because I want to try, too."

Reece hesitated, but he needed to ask. He'd heard what Carey had to say about the situation yesterday, but he wanted to hear what Sage thought of it, too. "What about Carey, though?"

Sage frowned. "What about him?"

Reece wasn't sure. "He's your mate. I don't want to take the bond away from the two of you. But I have to be honest. Even though I'm willing to try, I don't know if I can work in a threesome. I don't know if I can deal with everything that implies."

Sage slowly nodded. He didn't look angry, which was a relief, but it didn't help Reece read his expression. "I'm not sure I can make it work, either," Sage finally said.

Reece blinked. "But you seemed enthusiastic about it."

"Only because I finally got you to agree to give this a try. And I'll be honest, you're right. Carey is my mate, and I don't want to give up that bond. But I will if that's what you want. If you can't make it work, if you can't have both me and Carey in your life, I'll choose you."

Reece knew that was the truth, at least for now. But he also knew that Sage would easily fall in love with Carey. Their souls belonged together. They were perfect for each other, as perfect as anyone could be for someone else. It was the reason they were mates.

Reece, on the other hand, didn't share that bond with Carey. He wouldn't have the bond to mess up his feelings, and he wasn't sure he could fall in love with him. He wasn't sure he could stand watching Sage and Carey fall in love, either.

But he would try. He wouldn't allow them to fall in love with each other without falling in love with him. The worst thing he could do in the situation would be to isolate himself again.

He'd agreed to this. He'd agreed to date both Carey and Sage and to see where the threesome might go. That meant he had to be all in. He couldn't keep himself away from them. It was going to be a lot of hard work, especially with the memories still right there in his mind, with the fear of rejection and of being hurt again, but he could do this.

He deserved to be happy, even though he'd given up that happiness for so many years.

Emily wouldn't have wanted him to become a bitter old man. She would have wanted him to have a family, even if it wasn't with her and Sarah. She probably would slap him upside the head if she could right now.

But she couldn't. She was dead. She was in the past. While Reece would always cherish that past, it was time for him to look at the future, or at least, to try to.

And apparently, the future meant being with Carey and Sage.

Reece loved Sage. If this was the only way he could have him, he would deal with it. He would have to.

He reached out, offering Sage his hand, palm up. Sage had dropped his a little while ago, but Reece needed the contact again. He needed to feel Sage close.

Sage's eyes widened, but Sage didn't hesitate. He put his hand on top of Reece's.

Reece twisted them, linking their fingers together. He

cleared his throat. "Thank you."

"You don't have anything to thank me for."

Reece took a chance and raised Sage's hand to his lips. He kissed the back of it, and Sage's skin was as soft as he'd imagined. "Thank you for listening to me. For letting me talk. I've kept this secret inside for so long, I wasn't sure I could put it out there. But you gave me time, and so, thank you."

Sage's expression twisted. "We all have secrets. Of course I was going to listen to you. Just like you're going to listen to me when it's time for me to tell you mine."

Reece wasn't sure Carey had secrets. He was too much of a big mouth to be able to keep them. But he knew that Sage had one, and a big one at that. No one knew why he lived with the pack. No one knew what kind of shifter he was. The only one who was aware of all that information was Camden, and Reece suspected Sam, and maybe Toby. They were Sage's friends, so it would make sense that Sage had opened up to them. He hadn't told Reece because until now, Reece had pushed him away.

But he wouldn't do that anymore. Sage deserved to have him in his life, and he wanted to be his rock and hold him up when he needed him. So when Sage was ready, Reece would listen.

In the meantime, though, they had a date to go to.

CHAPTER FIVE

Sage wished he'd told Reece to stay with him, but they both needed a pause to get their thoughts together and relax. Still, talking to Reece had made him even more nervous about the date, and he'd spent the past hour pacing around his house until he finally had to leave to go to the restaurant.

He felt so, *so* sorry for Reece. He couldn't help but wonder if the three of them really could work, especially after what had happened to Reece. Sage could only imagine how hard life had been for him after he lost his mate and their daughter.

Gosh. Their *daughter.* Sage couldn't even imagine what Reece had gone through. It had to have been hell, and he'd been alone for all of that. It didn't matter that had it been at his hands. He might have pushed everyone away, but someone should have noticed. *Sage* should have noticed.

But he'd always known Reece the way he was now. Reece had already been back with the pack when Sage had moved in, so he hadn't known any differently. Everyone else had, though, and Sage would already be yelling at Frederic if he thought Reece wouldn't get angry at him for that.

But Reece had trusted him with his secret. He'd told him something he'd never told anyone else. Sage wasn't going to break the silent promise he'd made not to talk to anyone, even though his first instinct was to protect Reece against the world and the people who hadn't realized what was wrong with him. He would protect him better by keeping his mouth shut.

But it was hard. Not as hard as what Reece was still going through, but Sage wanted to help him, and he didn't know how. He wanted to do something, but he already knew that if he asked, Reece would push him away. He always did. He had until now, and it was a small miracle that he'd agreed to go on this date with Carey and Sage.

That was why Sage didn't know what would happen tonight. He wanted things to go well, but this information was a tiny piece in the puzzle that was Reece and that Sage hadn't had before, and now he understood Reece better. He understood why Reece was cautious, and he had even more doubts.

He supposed he was going to find out what would happen soon enough.

He waited until he couldn't wait any longer to head out to his car. He'd still be early at the restaurant, but he could sit in the car for a bit. He didn't want to continue pacing his house. He would start sweating — which was already a danger, considering how nervous he was — and that was the last thing he wanted.

What he wanted was to be perfect for Carey, but even more so, for Reece. He didn't want Reece to regret tonight, whatever happened. He hoped Reece would realize that they really could do this, but now that he knew what Reece had gone through, he would understand even better if Reece couldn't.

He would understand, but he would be destroyed.

He would still choose Reece, though. He hated thinking about that. He hated thinking about the pain he'd cause Carey, but there was no other way out of it for him. If Reece didn't want both of them, Sage would have to choose, and he already had. He'd chosen a long time ago, and unfortunately for Carey, there was nothing he could do about that. Sage had met Reece first. He'd fallen in love with Reece first.

That wouldn't change.

Sage drove to the restaurant, almost bouncing on his seat. Thoughts whirled in his head, and he needed to put them aside, at least for tonight. This evening was about the three of them, not about what had happened to Reece. Maybe eventually, Sage and Reece would talk about this again, but right now, Sage suspected that Reece wanted to have at least a few hours in which he didn't have to think about his dead mate and daughter.

It was still weird to imagine him as a mate and a father. Sage had never seen him in those roles, but maybe one day. Maybe one day, if the three of them could make it work, they could be a family. Sage had never thought about having children, and he didn't know if it was a good idea, especially considering Carey's personality, but it was something they might talk about in a year or two.

But first, the date had to go well, and Sage would do everything he could to make sure that happened.

He parked in front of the restaurant and smiled when he saw Reece's car. He wasn't surprised. Reece had probably come straight there after leaving Sage's house, just like Sage had been tempted to do. He'd decided to stay home only because he wanted a quiet place in which no one would be staring at him while he paced. But now both of them were here. Sage parked his car and left it, making a beeline for Reece, who was leaning against his car and looking at his phone.

Reece looked up just as Sage reached him, and his cheeks flushed.

That was such a rare event that Sage cherished the sight. He smiled at Reece and shuffled his feet, unsure what to say after what had happened earlier between them. Things felt slightly tense, slightly awkward, but then, they'd always been between them.

"You're early," they both said at the same time.

Sage snapped his mouth shut, and he looked at Reece, his eyes wide. Reece's lips were curling into a smile, and Sage couldn't help but mirror the expression.

Reece rubbed the back of his neck. "So that was awkward,"

he said.

"It was. I guess we're not used to seeing each other this way."

"You mean as a date. Yeah, it's a little weird. That's not the most awkward thing right now, though."

No, that was the conversation they'd had earlier. It hung between them, heavy with significance and emotions, and Sage didn't know if they could ignore it, or at the very least, step around it. He wanted to try, though. He didn't want this evening to be about what Reece had lost. He wanted it to be about what Reece could gain if he gave him and Carey a chance. "I'm grateful you talked to me," he began, trying to find a way to get Reece to understand that. "And I realize you don't want to talk about it again. We can ignore that conversation, at least for tonight. How does that sound?"

Reece's smile turned sad. "I wish I could forget it, but it's not easy."

"Oh, of course not. That's not what I meant. I know you'll never forget what happened to you, and I don't expect you to. I just meant that maybe for tonight, we could act as if you never came to talk to me. I don't want this evening to be awkward, or at least, no more than a first date should be. It's already going to be weird enough because there are three of us." Sage bit his lower lip. "And I haven't dated in years. Certainly not since I arrived here."

Reece cocked his head. "One day, you're going to tell me the story of how you moved here, right?"

"I'm going to have to." And Sage was going to have to tell him that he was an empath and a jackalope shifter.

But not tonight.

"I'm turning your words against you. You don't have to tell me anything you don't want to tell me."

Sage shrugged. "It's not as much that I don't want to tell you but rather that I'm not sure how you'll react, and I'm not looking forward to it. But it's something I don't want to talk about tonight." Sage forced himself to smile. "So. Is Carey already here?"

Reece shook his head. "He strikes me as the kind of guy who'd rather be later than early, to be honest. I'm not surprised to see he's not here yet."

"You might be right. What you think about him?"

Reece shrugged. "He's kind of weird, isn't he? I'm not trying to insult him or anything since he's your mate, but yeah."

Sage chuckled. "He might be my mate, but he's just a guy. You know that. If I had to choose between the two of you, I'll choose you. But yes, he's a little weird."

The smile on Reece's face finally widened and became a real one. "He might be good, for both of us."

"Yeah? How do you figure that?"

"Well, both of us tend to isolate ourselves, probably for very different reasons. He's exactly the opposite. He's outgoing and mouthy and noisy. Having him in our lives is going to be a huge change, and we're going to have to adapt. That probably means we won't be able to hide away, not as much as we're doing now."

Sage hadn't thought about that. He'd been so focused on what he could have with both Carey and Reece, but he hadn't thought about the consequences, not the ones unrelated to the two men. His life was about to change, whatever happened, whatever decision they made. It already was. He didn't quite know what to do with that, but that was okay. The three of them would find a way. Together.

Carey was late. Of course he was. He was always late, even tonight, which was one of the most important evenings of his life.

Sometimes, he wanted to kick his own ass.

"I'm going," he yelled through the house. He didn't know if anyone was home, since Lennox had gone out with Toby after the phone call with Douglas, but just in case, he wanted to be sure that no one would be looking for him.

He threw the door open and almost collided with Camden, the pack alpha and the man who was giving him and Lennox a place to stay for now. That would eventually change, since Carey was planning to get his own house with Reece and Sage, but it would be a while before that happened, and in the meantime, he was more than happy to have a room here.

He tried to sidestep Camden, who arched a brow and stayed right where he was. He looked Carey up and down, then asked, "What is it? Date night?"

Carey couldn't help but grin. "Damn right it is."

Camden's eyebrows rose high on his forehead. "You're not wasting time. And who's the lucky guy? Wait. Let me guess. I saw you talk to Sage at the party."

Carey's smile widened. He always smiled, but since he'd met Reece and Sage, he felt like he hadn't stopped. "Yep. Sage is my mate."

Camden's smile stayed where it was, but he frowned a little, which was an odd expression. "Sage is your mate."

"Yep, he is."

"I'm happy for you."

"But you know there's something between Sage and Reece, and you're not sure what's happening. That's okay. I'm actually dating both of them."

Camden blinked. "Both of them?"

Carey didn't have time to give Camden an explanation, but he felt he owed it to him. He was with the pack to protect Toby and Sam, which was what he and Lennox had been hired to do. Instead, he was going on a date, and he knew that wasn't what he was being paid for. "It won't distract me from my job, I promise."

Camden shook his head. "That's not what I was thinking. While it's true that you and Lennox are here to protect my mate and his brother, I don't expect you not to have a personal life. You're free to come and go, just like I told you already. I guess I'm surprised by the fact that you're dating both Reece *and* Sage. It's not something I expected."

"Trust me. I didn't expect that either. But I was so lucky that my mate is already in love with another guy. I get two guys for the price of one. Isn't it wonderful?" Carey looked at Camden as he spoke. He wanted to know if anyone was going to have a problem with them before it happened, especially if it came from the alpha. Camden had the power to kick the three of them out of the pack, and Carey didn't want that. He wasn't sure what he'd do if he did, but he would fight for Reece and Sage. This was their home. He didn't want that to be ripped away from them just because of him.

"I guess I'm just worried someone is going to get hurt. I know you're new, but you know Reece and Sage have . . . something. They have for a while."

"Oh, I know. They love each other." And Carey truly believed that if he hadn't barged in the picture, they would still be dancing around each other, nothing but friends. He didn't understand why they weren't dating already, but he would find out eventually. When it came to them, he would have patience.

"Well. That's all I had to say. Don't hurt anyone, and have fun," Camden said.

Carey *really* needed to go, but first, he wanted to reassure Camden. "I'm not out to hurt either Sage or Reece. I want both of them. I promise. I know it's weird, and that Sage is the only one who *is* my mate, but I don't care about that. I don't care about anything but the fact that I can have those two men in my life, and I can't wait for that to happen. I'm going to make them happy. I promise." Or, at the very least, Carey would do everything he could to make that happen.

Reece had to let him in, though. There could be no other way.

Camden clapped Carey's shoulder. "Well, I'll see you later, if you come home."

Carey wiggled his eyebrows. "I might not be the kind of guy who wants to wait, but I'm pretty sure Reece and Sage aren't ready for that step. But I'll see you later, yes. Wish me luck."

Then he was out the door before Camden could say anything else. He'd already wasted more than enough time. He was late, and it was getting worse by the minute.

He flirted with the speed limit all the way to the restaurant. He wasn't sure who had suggested coming here for their first date. Probably Sage, but now Carey wished the three of them had stayed in pack territory. Things were already going to be awkward as it was. Reece Sage could probably use a known environment so they would be more relaxed. But things were what they were, and Carey would have to deal with them.

So he did. He found the restaurant easily and parked his car, almost falling on his face in his haste to get out. He didn't have to look around to find Reece and Sage. He heard someone laugh when he almost fell, and he looked up to fake-glare. "Very funny. What would you have done if I had ended up with road-rash on my face?" he asked Sage, who was still snickering.

"You'd still be as gorgeous," Sage said. His cheeks were pink, and he looked lovely.

Carey couldn't stop smiling. "Of course I would be. I'm just like that. Gorgeous. Perfect."

Reece snorted. "That's what you think? That you're perfect?"

Carey wiggled his eyebrows at him. "Perfect enough that you agreed to go on a date with me."

Reece looked at the ground, clearly uncomfortable.

Great. Carey had already managed to embarrass him, and he wasn't sure what to do about it. He cleared his throat and looked around. "This looks like a nice place," he said.

"It is," Sage agreed. "And the food is good."

But they wouldn't be able to talk. There were a lot of people in the restaurant, a sign that Sage was probably right about the food, and while it would have been perfect any other day, Carey wanted to be able to talk to his two men. "Maybe we could wait to go in?" he asked.

Sage blinked at him. "You're not hungry?"

Carey grinned at him. "Not for food."

Sage's face flushed, and while Carey found it amusing and gorgeous, he didn't want Sage to feel uncomfortable. "What I meant is that I'd like to talk to you and Reece before we eat," he explained. "What do you think?"

"We could go for a walk," Reece suggested, and Carey was so surprised, he almost kissed the man.

"You want to go for a walk? With me?" he asked.

Reece rolled his eyes. His ears turned red and he looked away, and while Carey probably shouldn't find that endearing, he did. Reece was as adorable as Sage, even though they were so different.

It had to be weird for both of them, but especially for Reece. Sage and Carey shared the mate bond, but Reece didn't. He'd agreed to go on a date with them, but he could leave at any time. Sage could too, but it wouldn't be quite the same, because he and Carey would always share the bond.

That meant Carey had to work extra hard to make Reece see that he was welcomed. He wasn't lying when he'd said he wanted both of them in his life, and he was going to show that to them.

He gestured toward the sidewalk. "I know there's a park down there, right?" He hadn't explored Rosewood yet, but he'd driven through it a few times, so he knew approximately where they were.

"There is." Sage's expression brightened.

"We could head that way?" Hopefully, it would be mostly empty, since it was getting late in the evening. People were going home to have dinner, and this was a perfect moment to have a chat.

Things were still awkward between them, and while Carey didn't like it and wasn't used to it, he knew it was normal. This wasn't just a date with someone he liked. The rest of his future, his entire life, hinged on how this evening went. That was why he needed it to go perfectly.

The problem was that nothing was ever perfect in his life, and usually, he was the one who messed things up.

Things were awkward, to say the least, but Reece knew it was his fault, so he didn't say anything about it. He, Sage, and Carey were walking along a path in the park. Darkness had fallen around them, and it was almost as if they were alone in the universe. Or rather, it was as if Reece was alone. Sage and Carey walked next to each other. Their bodies were close as they talked. Carey was doing most of the talking, actually, but that was always the case with Sage. He was a good listener, but he didn't talk much.

It looked like Carey talked enough for both of them anyway.

Reece, on the other hand, was walking a few steps behind them. He was looking at them, wondering what was happening. He'd agreed to this date. But was this a good idea? Was this what he wanted in life?

He'd wanted Sage for years, but Carey was a surprise. Reece wasn't sure what to do with him. It was probably because he didn't know him well, but Carey was loud, and he seemed to always be happy. It wasn't something Reece was used to, and he didn't know if he could get used to it.

"Lennox is the quiet one," Carey was saying.

Reece had no trouble believing that.

"But we've been told that I talked enough for both of us, so it works, you know?"

"Well, you indeed talk a lot," Sage pointed out.

"I don't see why I shouldn't. There are so many things to talk about. Like, for example, what kind of shifter are you? Because I'm pretty sure you're not a wolf. It makes me wonder. Why do you live with the pack? Is it something like what happened with Toby and Sam? Are you a unicorn shifter, too?"

Reece's breath hitched. He wanted the answers to those questions, too, but he hadn't asked them until now, and he wasn't about to. Sage deserved his privacy, even when it came to something this important.

"I'm not a unicorn shifter," Sage said. His voice was quieter, and Reece found himself instinctively wanting to protect him. He didn't say anything, though. Sage and Carey were mates, and Carey deserved to know what kind of shifter Sage was even more so than Reece.

"Is it a secret, then? Because I promise I won't tell anyone."

"It *is* kind of a secret, mostly because I'm sure that some people would come after me if they knew I lived here. That's why Camden agreed not to tell anyone."

"But Reece and I are your boyfriends. You're safe with us." Carey looked back, and only now seemed to realize that Reece was behind them rather than walking with them. He stopped in the middle of the path and turned to face Reece, and Sage followed his lead.

Carey crossed his arms over his chest and cocked his head. "What are you doing?" he asked Reece.

Reece stopped in front of him. "What are you talking

about? I'm walking right along with you."

"No, you're not. You're walking behind us. You're giving us time to be together and to get to know each other."

"Isn't that exactly what you wanted? Isn't that why you asked us on a date?"

Carey shook his head. "I asked you *both* on this date. Yes, I do want to get to know Sage, but I also want to get to know you, and I'm not right now. You've been so quiet that if I didn't know you were here, I wouldn't know you were."

Reece blinked. "Does that even make sense?"

Carey shrugged. "You know what I mean, so yes, it does. What's going on? Are you regretting this?"

Reece bit the inside of his cheek. He wasn't regretting the date, but it was true that he wasn't quite sure what to do. "It's just weird."

"Talk to us, then. We can't deal with the weirdness if you don't say anything about it. What's weird? Me?"

Reece rubbed his forehead. "It's you, and Sage, and I haven't been on a first date in more than fifteen years. And you ask a lot of questions, but I'm not about to tell you my entire life story just because you want to find out about it."

"I don't expect you to tell me everything you've been through tonight. It's obvious something bad happened to you, and I'm sorry. I'm here if you want to talk to me. I'm not going to ask, though. You're not comfortable with it, and that's good enough for me. Why don't you ask questions, then?"

"You have to make an effort," Sage said softly. "I know it's hard."

He would know, since Reece had told him about Emily and Sarah. He knew exactly how hard this was, and Reece was grateful he wasn't pushing as hard as Carey was.

But Carey was right. Reece had agreed to this. He'd agreed to give a relationship with both men a try, and he wasn't doing it. He decided to, yet he was already backing down, and he didn't like that.

He'd been backing down for the past fifteen years. He'd been living his life, or rather, surviving, for all those years. It was time for a change. He was the only one who could make that change, though, and he had to make an effort, no matter how awkward and weird it made him feel.

He swallowed. "I'll tell you eventually," he told Carey. "I'm looking forward to it. It was the worst experience of my life, and Sage and Frederic are the only ones who know. But if we're going to do this, I need to trust you. I'm going to have to tell you my secrets."

"I'm a jackalope shifter," Sage suddenly blurted out.

Reece and Carey both looked at him. Carey cocked his head as if he were trying to read Sage, but Reece had questions. "Jackalope?" He hadn't even known those actually existed.

Sage bit his lower lip. "You know. Like a rabbit, but with horns."

"I know what a jackalope is. I just wasn't aware you guys were real."

To Reece's surprise, Sage glared at him. "Unicorns exist. Why shouldn't jackalopes?"

Carey barked out a laugh. "He has a point. You know unicorn shifters. You know phoenix shifters. What do you have against jackalopes?"

Reece could already tell Carey was going to drive him crazy if they did this, but for some reason, instead of dreading it, he was looking forward to it. Carey's presence made his heart race, and while he wasn't sure why, now wasn't the time to examine those feelings. "I don't have anything against jackalope shifters or any shifter. I'm just surprised." It did make sense, though. Just like unicorn and phoenix shifters, jackalope shifters were extremely rare. It also explained why Sage was on the run.

"What's your gift?" Reece asked.

Sage's chin dipped down. "I should have told you a long time ago."

Reece could already tell he wasn't going to like it, but coming from Sage, he would accept just about anything. "You don't have to tell us if you don't want to."

"I'm an empath. I can feel other people's emotions. I can feel yours, and Carey's. I'm trying hard to block them out, but some are strong." Sage looked Reece in the eyes. "You're in love. You're confused. There's always a bit of pain that mingles with the other feelings you have. I know why now."

Reece took a step back. "You can feel my emotions."

"I've always been able to."

"That means you knew. You knew I love you."

Sage rubbed his hands on his thighs. "I did. I'm sorry, and I would have stopped if I could have, but I don't control it. I can try blocking, but when you feel strongly about something, there's not much I can do. I can't switch off my gift, not the way Toby and Sam can. I never told you about it because I didn't want you to feel like I was breaking your trust."

Reece might not be sure what this meant for the three of them, but he didn't want Sage to feel bad about this, so he moved toward him, reaching for Sage and hoping he would respond. "It's fine. I was surprised. That's all. I'm not angry with you, I promise."

Reece was relieved when Sage stepped closer, and he wrapped an arm around Sage's shoulders. "Thank you for trusting us."

"See," Carey exclaimed. "This is what I was talking about. We're getting to know each other. We're cuddling."

Reece rolled his eyes. "We're not cuddling. I'm hugging Sage."

Carey's smile widened when he moved closer, too. He

wrapped his arms around Reece and Sage's waists and pulled them close. He reached up and pressed their lips together, then smacked his lips against Sage's, too.

Reece's first kiss since Emily, and this was how it happened.

"I like this," Carey said.

And to Reece's surprise, he did, too.

CHAPTER SIX

Things were going well. Sage hadn't expected that when he, Carey, and Reece had started dating a few weeks ago. So far they'd only gone on a few dates, because they were taking things slow. Sage and Reece especially needed time, but it felt like things were finally coming together. Sage hoped it would continue that way, because he wasn't sure what he'd do if he lost either Carey or Reece.

He wanted them both.

He'd been hesitant when Carey had suggested this solution, but now he was sure of it. He wanted to be with both his men, and things would work out. They had to.

Reece was the most hesitant of the three of them, and Sage understood. He hadn't told Carey about his past yet, and Carey hadn't pushed, which was great. Eventually, though, Reece would have to tell Carey, and other people too, like Camden. Camden especially would be disappointed that Reece hadn't confided in him. Sage had been somewhat, even though he knew where Reece was coming from.

He'd lost a mate and a child. That kind of wound was almost impossible to come back from. It was a small miracle that Reece was still with them, that he was still coherent. That he was giving Sage and Carey a chance. Sage wasn't sure what he would do if he lost either of his men. He would probably close down and isolate himself from the world even more than he already was.

Something poked at his leg, and he looked up at Carey. Carey was still poking at him with his foot while licking his ice cream and staring.

Sage shook his head. "I'm sorry." He and Carey had met for ice cream while Reece was working. Sage had been hesitant to accept, especially when Carey had asked him in front of Reece, but Reece had just told them that he wished he could come, but he had work to do, and to have fun and eat some ice cream for him, too.

Sage had no experience with threesomes. He wasn't sure how they would be able to find a balance, how Reece felt about being at work while Carey and Sage were having fun, but he knew they would have to talk about it.

"What's going on in that head of yours?" Carey asked.

Sage contemplated not telling him, but Carey was the one who always pushed to talk. He also was the only one of them who had experience with this, so he probably knew better than Sage what they should do.

Sage leaned back in his seat. "I'm just wondering what Reece is doing and how he's feeling about this."

Carey gave another lick to his ice cream. "I see. What do you think he's doing?"

"Working. Obviously."

"Obviously. And how do you think he feels about the two of us being out on a date alone?"

Sage shook his head. "I don't know. I wish I did, though. You know he's the most hesitant about this, and I'm afraid that this is going to ruin everything."

Carey took his time before answering. "It certainly can. One of the main reasons my throuples have imploded was jealousy. I won't deny that."

"How much experience do you have with having more than one person in your life? Because you make it sound like it's a lot."

Carey laughed. He always seemed to laugh, smile, or generally be happy, and Sage wasn't quite sure what to do with that. He liked it, though. "Not as much experience as you seem to think. But I've been in a few throuples, so I feel I know what I'm talking about."

"Why do you enjoy this kind of relationship so much?"

"It's not that I enjoy this kind of relationship, although I do. It's that I don't believe in monogamy. I don't believe in loving only one person for the rest of your life. That's not how it works. I'm faithful in all my relationships, of course, but I think that expecting people to be with only one person is limiting and unrealistic. I like you. I like Reece. Why should I have to choose if we can make things work this way?"

He wasn't wrong, but Sage only knew couples. Even though the Rosewood pack was accepting and didn't have a problem with the alpha being gay, for example, there weren't other throuples. He, Reece, and Carey were pioneers, and it wasn't easy. "What about the people who don't accept the way you think?"

"I don't get into relationships with them." Carey huffed. "I get what you mean. You're right. Some people think that what we're doing is wrong. Does it really matter, though? As long as the three of us are happy and in love, why should we care about what the people say?"

"It's easy to say that when you're new here. But this is Reece's pack, and even I've been here for years. I don't want people to hate me just because I have two men in my life."

Carey tapped his fingertips on the table. "Even though Lennox and I don't exactly have a family anymore, we do have a flock. Some people like us." He paused and grinned. "Well, *some* people like *me*. Most don't seem to mind Lennox, but that's because he doesn't speak at all. But you get what I mean. Do I want everyone to like me? Of course I do. I don't think anyone wants to be disliked. But I also know it's not realistic to expect everyone to always agree with me. I tend to rub people the wrong way, and that's fine. I have Lennox, and now, I have you and Reece. I have the pack, or at the very least, Camden and Toby, and Sam and Frederic. It's more people than I've had in a long time, and I'm happy. Besides, I'm sure that those people in the pack who don't like what we're doing will have to get used to the idea, because I'm not going anywhere, and you aren't, either. And I know Camden well enough to know that he will kick people's asses if they have anything to say about this."

That was the truth. Camden wouldn't accept bigotry, which was one of the reasons Sage had decided to settle here. "I'm trying to accept this."

"But it's hard. I get it, which is why I haven't pushed for more. For the moment, I'm happy with dating you and Reece. I can't wait to take you out again. Maybe just the two of us? I feel that we have to get to know each other and that he's not exactly comfortable with me."

Sage chuckled. "I'm pretty sure it has nothing to do with you."

"You talk to him more than you do to me. Is it still the bond that annoys him?"

"It doesn't annoy him. I think he's puzzled by how accepting you are of him being in this relationship with us."

"And you?"

"I was in the beginning." But Sage was starting to understand what Carey was talking about.

He was right. Sage had never loved two people at the same time, but that was mostly because he'd never loved anyone before he'd fallen in love with Reece. But now he loved Reece, and he had feelings for Carey, too. It wasn't love yet, but he could see how it could become love.

He didn't have to choose. He had feelings for two men, and he could have both in his life. He wished that people knew it was a possibility, and that others didn't hate their solution. Why did they care about it anyway? As long as they weren't the ones in a throuple, why *should* they care?

"So." Carey said. "Why don't you tell me about your past? So far, I only know that you're a jackalope shifter. That's not a lot."

The only thing Sage could feel coming from Carey was curiosity, underlined with affection, so he knew Carey didn't want to use his empathy. He was just curious. "As you know, all jackalope are empaths, but some are stronger than others. I was one of the strongest in the colony. The alpha used me ever since I was a kid, and I didn't know any better, so I went along with it. It was mostly for business stuff."

"But you're not part of the colony anymore. What happened?"

"I don't like to think about it, but you have to know, I guess. Reece does, too." And maybe Sage should tell both of them at the same time, but he didn't think Reece would mind. Reece understood and accepted a lot more than he admitted. He knew the three of them shared a bond and that there was no reason to be jealous.

Sage hadn't realized it until now, but if he thought of Reece and Carey together without him, he wasn't jealous. He wanted them to be in love with each other. He wanted them to want to be in this relationship as much as he did.

He cleared his throat. "I ran away. I had to. Once I turned eighteen, I started looking for another solution. I was of legal age, and I'd had enough of doing that stuff. I was old enough to leave the colony anytime I wanted. My alpha didn't like it. He locked me up after threatening me and tried to keep me in his house. But the worst part was when he decided to sell me off after my father died."

Carey's smile faded. "Sell you off?"

"The only reason he kept me in the first place was that I was convenient and useful, but also because my father had refused to allow him to do anything to me. When my father died, the alpha decided I could be used to enter an alliance with a nearby bear sleuth. They could have decimated us if they'd wanted to, and even though the colony was always small, we were still all jackalope shifters. We were precious to most shifters. That was the way the alpha thought he could save the colony. By selling me off. I managed to escape the night before I was supposed to leave."

"Give me his name. Tell me where he is, and I'll kill him for you."

Sage should probably have been horrified about that, but instead, he laughed. "I don't want you to kill him. I never want to go back. I don't care what happens to him. It's not my problem anymore."

But he had people who loved him. He knew that if he told Reece the story, he would react the same way.

Reece and Carey loved Sage, and that was all Sage had been looking for.

Carey wanted to find out who had hurt Sage and kick his ass, but he could tell that Sage wouldn't tell him. It was just as well. He knew that was the last thing their relationship needed, and besides, he was on the job. He and Lennox were here to protect Toby and Sam. Even though Camden hadn't said anything about Carey going on dates and settling down with the pack, Carey knew that leaving Rosewood would be a bit much even for him, especially if it was for that reason. Camden had to know what had happened to Sage. From what Sage had said, he was the only one who was aware of his back story.

But maybe someday. Maybe Carey would be able to convince someone to give him a name, and once he had it, no one would be able to stop him from going to Sage's colony and let them know what he thought about them. The fact that Sage hadn't mentioned that anyone outside his father who'd stood up for him didn't sit well with Carey, and he would make sure that never happened again. From now on, Sage would always have someone to protect him, to talk for him when he couldn't. Carey would make sure of that, and he knew that Reece would, too.

Carey knew better than most what it was like not to have anyone, but even he had always had Lennox. Sage didn't have brothers, or at least, Carey didn't think so. If he did, they hadn't tried to stop what had happened, so he might as well not have them. But now he had two boyfriends, and Carey knew that he and Reece would do everything they could to make Sage happy and to make sure that nothing like that happened again.

Sage reached over the table and gently touched Carey's arm. "I'm touched that you want to do that, but you don't have to. It's in the past. It's been a while, and I'm safe now. I've been safe since I arrived in Rosewood. I just want to forget what happened. I want to focus on the future with you and Reece. Maybe you should do the same. I don't want to lose you because you were impulsive and decided to go after my past."

Carey gave his ice cream an angry lick. "I'm not going anywhere." But he was angry.

Sage leaned back in his chair, a satisfied smile playing on his lips. "Thank you. And honestly, the way you're reacting is more than enough for me to feel better. Camden wasn't happy when I told him about it, of course, but he's the alpha. He couldn't do anything except give me a place to stay, which was more than enough. He kept me safe and gave me a home, and I owe him a lot."

"He's a good man." Carey peered at Sage above his ice cream. "No one here knows what kind of shifter you are except for him, right? You said something like that the other day."

"You're right. Considering what I can do, I thought it would be better if no one found out. I trust the pack, but there's nothing to say that one of them, or even a stranger, wouldn't see me and decide to use me, or worse, to sell me like my alpha tried to do. I'm not ready to put my entire life at risk, not again. Not when I have so much more to lose this time around."

Carey wrinkled his nose. "So how does it work? You don't shift?"

"I do. But I stick to my house. I'm a small shifter anyway, so there's more than enough space for me to move around inside."

That was sad. Sage was a shifter, and his animal side deserved to be free as much as his human was. Sage wasn't entirely wrong when he said that there was more than enough space in his house for him to move around, but it couldn't be the same as hopping around the forest. Carey was sure of that, and he wanted to change it. "What would you think about going to the forest and shifting?" he asked, excitement building.

Sage frowned. "It's not safe."

"I'll keep you safe. You trust me, right?"

"Of course."

This was it. Carey rose from his chair, threw away what remained of his ice cream, and took Sage's hand, dragging him to his feet. Sage's eyes were wide, but he didn't protest, and he didn't try to stop Carey as Carey tugged him toward the car.

"Where are we going?" Sage asked once they were inside.

Carey was already driving. "Home."

"Oh? Did I say something wrong?"

"Of course not. We're going to the forest. We're going to shift, and I'll make sure that you're safe and that no one sees you. You're not alone anymore, Sage. You have Reece and me, and we'll protect you." That sounded like a perfect idea, so instead of parking in front of Camden's house, Carey parked in front of Reece's, then hopped up the porch steps to knock on his door.

Reece worked from home, which was a good thing. He looked edible when he opened the front door wearing sweat-pants and a t-shirt, his feet bare. He scowled at Carey, but the scowl softened when he saw Sage coming up behind him. "What are the two you doing here? I thought you went out for ice cream?"

Carey beamed. No matter how hard Reece tried to fake be-ing annoyed with him, Carey knew he wasn't. Well, maybe he was, but not seriously.

Things between them would always be a bit harder than they were between either of them and Sage. Carey was aware of that. Their personalities didn't mesh together quite as well as they did with Sage's, but that was okay. They didn't have to. Carey liked that he and Reece were so different.

"I'm taking Sage in the forest to shift. Did you know that he's never shifted there since he arrived in Rosewood? He usually sticks to his house."

Reece's eyes widened, and he looked at Sage. "Is that true?"

Sage nodded, not looking at Reece. "I couldn't risk it," he murmured.

"So I thought we could take him there and that we could protect him while he shifts. That way, we can make sure noth-ing happens to him," Carey said. He hoped Reece would be on board with that. He realized that Reece had work to do, but surely he could take a half an hour break to come running with them. Not that Carey would run — he was a bird shifter, so he flew — but they could play around for a bit. It would be good for all of them, and it might help further their relationship. It couldn't hurt.

Reece took a step back, and to Carey's relief, he reached for a pair of shoes in the entrance. "I'm in. It's probably more than time for me to shift anyway. I tend to forget to do it when I'm busy, and between my job and the two of you, I've been too busy lately," he said as he stepped out of the house and closed the door.

Carey couldn't help the winning grin that spread on his face. "Great. Let's go, then." He hopped off the steps that led the way, relieved when both Reece and Sage followed him.

"So, the thing you're most afraid of is that someone will see you?" he asked Sage as they walked deeper into the forest.

"I know that no one in the pack would hurt me, but yeah. I've had bad experiences, as you know, and they happened with people who should have protected me. I couldn't risk it."

"But now you have Reece and me, and we'll protect you."

"I know. It's still a bit weird, though. It's been so long since I shifted in a place that wasn't my house."

Once they were far enough away, Carey stopped in the middle of the forest and turned to face Sage. "Go ahead. We'll be right here, keeping an eye out."

Sage looked at him for a moment, then, to Carey's surprise, started to strip. Carey averted his eyes, and his gaze collided with Reece's, who was doing the same thing. Reece cautiously smiled at Carey, and Carey's heart swelled in his chest. They were doing this. They were working together as a throuple, and Carey couldn't have been happier.

Something tugged on his jeans, and he looked down to find Sage looking at him, his jackalope form about the size of an ordinary rabbit.

Carey laughed. "You're gorgeous," he said, crouching down and rubbing one of Sage's horns.

He could have sworn that Sage grinned at him, but of course, Sage was a jackalope right now, so he couldn't smile.

He hopped away, throwing himself into a small pile of leaves, squeaking in pleasure.

"Thank you," Reece murmured. He was staring at Sage, and he looked wistful.

"What are you thanking me for?" Carey wasn't sure, and he didn't want to assume.

"For doing this. I never realized he wasn't shifting as much as he could and that he kept it to his house. I should have. It's not right for him to not be able to do this out here."

"Well, that's why you have me. So I can see things that you can't." Carey truly believed that, and he hoped Reece was starting to understand it.

He wanted the three of them to complete each other, and this felt like one more step toward that goal.

Reece should've known. He should have realized what was going on with Sage a long time ago. He'd been too lost in his pain, but that was over now.

The pain wasn't, of course. Reece doubted it ever would be over, considering how long it had been. He still felt the same, although it didn't hurt as badly. The pain had gone from searing holes in his chest to being a twinge when he allowed himself to think about it, especially now that he had Sage and Carey. It was easier for him to focus on things that weren't what he'd lost, but rather, what he could have had.

But he still should have seen it. He should have understood that Sage was hiding.

The pack didn't have the habit of shifting together, but more often than not, Reece stumbled on several of them when he went out to run in his wolf form. He usually shifted with Frederic, and now, with Sam, too. He'd asked Sage if he wanted to come a few times, but Sage had always refused, and now, Reece knew why.

He hadn't been shifting in the forest. He had been hiding, and Reece hated that.

But not anymore. Thanks to Carey, Sage was free to hop around the way he was now, and it was a pleasure to watch.

"I should have known," he murmured.

Carey patted his arm. "I don't think you could have. Sage was very careful not to let anyone find out about this. And that's why the three of us are going to work, isn't it?"

Reece couldn't help but smile. "What do you mean?"

"I truly think we complete each other. We think about things differently. We see things differently because we had different experiences, and that's exactly why this will work. Each of us is going to bring something different to our relationship."

Reece understood, and he *hoped*. He hadn't allowed himself to hope in fifteen years, and he prayed he wouldn't be wrong about this.

Because he wanted it. He'd made sure to keep himself slightly separate from Sage and Carey, just in case something happened. He wanted them to get to know each other so he'd be sure that they wouldn't leave him behind. Both of them had insisted that wouldn't happen, but Reece couldn't help but think it might.

That conviction was fading a little more every day, though. Sage was still a bit shy, but he was more affectionate with Reece than he'd have been. And Carey, well, no one would say that Carey was shy. He didn't hesitate—not for anything—not even when Reece tried to push him away. He'd forced his way inside Reece's life, and he'd dragged Sage along with him, and now they were there to stay.

Reece liked it. He hadn't thought he would, but now that he had them, he wouldn't change things for anything. Their relationship was by no means perfect, and he doubted it ever would be, but it was better than the searing loneliness he'd forced on himself until now.

He couldn't believe that it had only taken one man, but that was the reality of it. Carey had barged into his life, and now, he wouldn't leave, even if Reece wanted him to.

And he didn't.

An arm slipped around his waist, and he jerked. Carey grinned at him, not one bit offended. He always gave Reece time to wrap his mind around what was happening without being pushy or demanding. He might be a loudmouth, and he might seem like a person who didn't think before he acted, but that wasn't true. Carey thought about a lot of things. He made sure he never hurt neither Sage nor Reece. He was thoughtful and smart, even though he liked to act like he wasn't.

"We're really doing this," Carey said.

He was right, and Reece needed to let go. Emily and Sarah would always be part of his life, but now the most important people for Reece were Carey and Sage. He had to focus on them. He had to let go of the guilt. He had to think about the future, not about the past.

He surprised even himself when he leaned closer to Carey and kissed his cheek. Carey's eyes widened, as did his smile. When Reece tried to step away, he hung on, hooking an arm around Reece's neck and pulling him close again. He pressed their lips together, and even though it hurt a bit because their teeth collided, Reece was happy. This was Carey — enthusiastic, energetic, open, and unhesitant. When he wanted something, he asked, and he generally got it.

It had worked with Reece.

They kissed, and it was easy enough not to think about Emily. Kissing Carey was nothing like kissing her had been, and Reece was grateful he couldn't make comparisons.

It was deeper than any kiss he and Carey had exchanged, and Reece allowed himself to sink into it. The three of them hadn't tumbled into bed yet, but it would happen, and soon. Reece knew that they all wanted it. They were still working their way around each other, but they wanted it to happen, even though at least in his case, Reece wasn't sure how. He'd never been with more than one person, or even with a guy. He wasn't quite sure about the logistics of three guys together, but he would find out, and Carey would be an enthusiastic teacher.

Something pulled on Reece's sweats, and he chuckled, looking down to find Sage trying to pull him away from Carey. He knew Sage wasn't jealous. Reece was, sometimes, but it was fairly easy to focus on how happy Sage was to forget that emotion.

They shouldn't be jealous of each other. Reece wanted Sage to be happy, and that was what Carey was doing. He made Sage happy, and now, Reece, too. Reece wouldn't have thought it possible a few months ago, but now, he couldn't deny that was what was happening.

"What do you think?" Carey asked, his arms still wrapped around Reece. He was breathing heavily, and Reece couldn't help but smile smugly at the thought that he'd been the one to do that. "Shall we shift, too?"

"Yes, please." Reece couldn't wait to see Carey's form. Sage was an adorable bundle of fur, but he knew that Carey would be majestic. He'd never seen a phoenix shifter in their phoenix form, and he couldn't wait. He, on the other hand, was a normal wolf, so nothing exciting, but the thought of spending some time with both Carey and Sage, playing around the forest and forgetting about everything else, felt good. They all needed it.

Carey's smile widened — he was always smiling, whatever happened, but his best smiles were reserved for Sage and Reece — and pulled off his t-shirt. Reece's eyes widened, but he should have known better than to think Carey would want to hide. He wasn't shy. He didn't care who saw him, and Reece suspected that in this case, he was more than happy to show off his body.

He was beautiful. He was taller than Sage but shorter than Reece. His shoulders were wide, but even though the three of them were so different, or maybe *because* they were, he was gorgeous. His muscles rippled as he moved, and Reece wasn't surprised to see the phoenix tattooed on his back. He arched a brow at Carey, who just shrugged. "I know. It's predictable, but I don't care. I love it."

So did Reece, even though the tattoo didn't stand a chance when he finally saw Carey in his phoenix form.

He'd been right. Carey was majestic. His feathers were a riot of colors going from deep red to bright yellow. He almost looked like a flying fire, and Reece was afraid to touch him. He knew Carey's feathers wouldn't burn him, but they were so bright. They weren't hot, though. They were smooth, and they moved under his fingertips with every movement Carey made.

Then Carey took flight. He made a sound, almost like a song, and flew in circles above their heads. He seemed to be telling Reece to get a move on and shift, too, and Reece obeyed.

It had been a while since he'd felt so light and free. He hadn't allowed himself to be, but he doubted he would have even if he had. He'd let the memories keep him back from life.

But things were different now. He had Carey and Sage, and even though he'd fought against their presence in his life in the beginning, he was grateful that one. He knew things could work between them, but only if he had allowed them to.

And he would. He had to because he wanted this. He wanted to be happy, and he wanted to be happy with Sage *and* Carey.

CHAPTER SEVEN

They were in bed together.

It was weird. Sage had never shared a bed, and now here he was, with one man on his right, and another man on his left. Things were tense between the three of them, no matter how many jokes Carey cracked. Sage had thought this was a good idea when Carey had suggested it, and Reece had agreed, but now, they might as well be three pieces of wood under a blanket.

Carey huffed. "This isn't working. Why isn't it working?"

Sage shook his head. "I'm not sure."

Carey propped himself up on his elbow and looked down at Sage, then at Reece. "It's my fault. I shouldn't have pushed. But we were going so good after playing in the forest that I thought this might be a good idea." He grimaced. "Obviously, I was wrong."

Sage wasn't used to seeing Carey so unsure, and he didn't like it. Carey was a force of nature. He rushed down his path once he made a decision, and he didn't hesitate to drag people down with him as he went. Yet this time, he looked like he might be about to run, and Sage didn't want that to happen.

He pushed a hand between Carey and the mattress so he could give him a half-hug without having to move away from Reece. "It's the first time we've done this. It's obvious we're a bit nervous."

Carey flopped back into the mattress and snuggled against Sage's side.

That was new, too. Although Sage had been on the run

from his colony for a while and wasn't a virgin anymore, he'd always been the little spoon. He'd always been the one who got fucked. Carey didn't seem to have a problem snuggling up to him, though. He didn't seem to care that Sage was smaller and slighter than him. If people saw them together, they would assume that Carey was the dominant one in the bedroom, yet he looked more like a puppy right now. A *kicked* puppy.

"We had fun in the forest," Reece said. He was on his back, staring at the ceiling.

Sage smiled. "I agree. Thank you. It had been a while, and I realize now that I waited too long," Sage said.

Reece rolled his head on his pillow to look at him. "Why did you? I mean, I know you couldn't tell anyone what kind of shifter you are, but if you'd come to me, I would have looked the other way while keeping you safe while you shifted."

"But it wouldn't have been fair to you."

Reece reached out and stroked a fingertip down Sage's jaw. "Why not? I would have been more than happy to do it. You're not alone, Sage. You weren't before, either, although I admit that I wasn't the best at showing you that."

He hadn't been, but he was getting better. Now that they were talking instead of staring at the ceiling, Sage was relaxing, and he could feel that Carey and Reece were, too. "You know, we shouldn't be so awkward. We should forget it and do what we want."

"I don't want to push too hard." Carey wrinkled his nose. "I always do, and I don't want to mess this up. This relationship is important to me. I know I come off as uncaring and flighty, but I'm not. I want the three of us to work. It's the most important thing for me right now, and that's not going to change anytime soon."

To Sage's surprise, it was Reece who answered. "You don't

have to walk around on eggshells with us. We both know how you are, and neither of us thinks you're stupid or anything like that. You might be a *little* flighty, but you also know when to be serious. Our relationship is important to the three of us, and we need to do this together."

"Reece is right," Sage agreed. "And I know that first times are usually awkward, but this really shouldn't be. Or rather, even though it is, we should work through it and get past it. Besides, it's okay to be awkward, isn't it? We have a lot of time to learn to be with each other. This is only the beginning."

"So what do we do now?" Carey asked.

Sage laughed. He couldn't help it. "Well, it was your idea to come back to my house and to get in bed together. What do you want to do?"

Carey wiggled his eyebrows. "What do you *think* I want to do? You two are hot. I've wanted in your pants since the first time I saw you at the party, and that hasn't changed. I doubt it's going to change for a long, *long* time. That's what I was hoping when I suggested this, but I didn't think about how awkward it might be."

"But like Sage said, it doesn't *have* to be awkward," Reece murmured.

"It's going to be, though," Sage said. "I mean, look at us. Neither you nor I have had a relationship in fifteen years. I've had sex more recently, but it was nowhere close to what this is. I don't know what to do. I mean, physically, I know, of course. But this isn't just physical. There are a lot of feelings involved, and it's overwhelming."

"How about we forget about feelings?" Carey asked. "I mean, not that you have to stop being in love or anything, but why don't we go with what we feel like doing? You're right, Sage. That's probably the only way to make this less awkward." He reached over, wrapping an arm around Reece's waist, and pulling him close. That move meant that Sage was sandwiched between the two men, and he had to roll to his side so they could get even closer.

He had Reece at his back and Carey at his front. He sucked in a breath, but to his surprise, instead of kissing him, Carey reached around him and kissed Reece.

It was incredibly sexy. Sage couldn't have imagined how much until he saw it, and now he wondered how he'd managed to live without this for so long. The answer to that was easy. The only reason he was comfortable with being with two guys right now was that those two guys were Reece and Carey.

And together, they were better than watching porn.

Sage ran his hands over every inch of skin he could get to, both Carey's and Reece's. It was slightly awkward in Reece's case because he was behind him, but that only meant that Sage could push his ass back against Reece's cock.

Reece groaned, a sound that came from deep in his throat, and he thrust forward, his cock thickening and pushing between Sage's ass cheeks.

"How is this going to work?" Sage asked, sounding breathless. He felt breathless, too.

"However you want it to work," Carey answered as he stopped kissing Reece and pressed his lips to Sage's collarbone. He kissed a path down Sage's chest, and when Reece pulled Sage so he could roll to his back, Sage went without a protest. Why should he protest? This was what he wanted, even though he hadn't known he wanted it.

He rolled, and Reece kissed him. It was hard to focus on one thing with two pairs of lips and hands torturing him, and Sage realized he didn't have to. He only had to feel, and that was what he did. He closed his eyes and didn't try to understand who was doing what anymore. He didn't care who he was touching, who was kissing his throat, who was sucking on his nipple. It didn't matter. He knew that eventually he'd be able to learn how different Reece and Carey's touches were, but this was too new for him, and maybe that was what made it perfect.

He didn't know who was doing what, and that meant that he couldn't treat Reece and Carey differently. That was what their relationship needed. The three of them had to be equals, and even though making that happen would take a lot of work, Sage was more than happy to put that work in to make sure the relationship worked.

Carey needed to be especially careful with Reece. He was the one who was more hesitant, and it made sense. Carey knew enough of Reece's past now to understand. He was still hurting, and anything could remind him of his past and his mate.

Carey didn't want that to happen. He wanted their first time to be perfect, even though there was no such thing as a perfect first time. Things were always slightly awkward, and there was a lot of hesitating and wondering, but they could get through this, and once they did, they would be more comfortable with each other.

But even if something happened, if one of them came too soon or gave someone an elbow in the face, things would still be perfect because he was doing this with Reece and Sage.

He was falling in love with them—with *both* of them.

He could see the three of them living in Sage's house eventually. He wouldn't think twice about moving in, but he understood that for Reece, it was different. He had his little house, and he'd lived there for seven years. From what Carey knew, it had been his parents' before they moved away to another pack when they retired. It was his now, and it had a lot of meaning for him. It had been his safe place during the past seven years. It would take a lot for him to move out, but maybe it would be a good thing for him. Maybe that was what he needed to get over his past.

Not that Carey wanted him to get over it. He didn't want Reece to forget his past and the people who had been important to him. But they were starting a future together, and Carey wanted their relationship to be about that. He wanted Reece to think about them, not about the loss and pain.

"Who's doing what, then?" Sage asked.

Carey laughed. "Does it matter? We can do what we feel like doing?"

"Maybe, but I'd like to know what you like in bed. Do you like to, you know, be the receiver, or do you like it the other way around?"

Carey laughed again. Sage was precious and adorable. "You mean if I like to fuck or be fucked?"

Sage's cheeks reddened, even though he was naked between two men just as naked and had been for a while. "Yes. That's what I was talking about. And the same goes for you, Reece."

Reece shook his head. "I don't know. I've never done this with a guy."

Carey blinked. "But you're gay."

"Bisexual."

His tone didn't bode well, so Carey decided not to push for more answers. Besides, it had been a stupid observation, since Reece's mate had been a woman. "Okay, then you can find out with us. Since I'm the one with more experience in this case — and guys, I don't want you to get offended by that — I think we should stick to something pretty simple." Mostly, he couldn't wait to get back to kissing Sage or Reece. It didn't matter who. "No penetration this time around. We should talk about that first." He didn't want either of his men to freak out while they were getting busy.

This bed was theirs, and they were supposed to be comfortable in it, both physically and mentally. Reece was already tense because of the question Carey had asked, and Carey didn't want to continue along that line.

He reached and pulled Reece close to kiss him. "I'm sorry if I said something that offended or angered you," he murmured.

"It doesn't matter. It's my problem, not yours."

"It might be your problem, but since we're together, it's going to become our problem, too. But I understand that now is probably not the best moment to talk about it. That's okay." He kissed Reece again, smiling when Sage rolled to his other side and kissed Reece's chest.

Maybe *this* was how things could work. So far, Carey and Reece had focused on Sage. He was the one who'd brought them together. But maybe they should focus on Reece instead. *He* was the unsure one. He was the one who felt left out. He was the one who might run at any second, and Carey didn't want that to happen.

So he and Sage both focused on Reece. They pushed him to his back, and Sage climbed on top of him, straddling his thighs and looking down at him. Carey scooted closer, pressing his side against Reece's, sucking his nipple between his lips and lightly biting on it.

Reece groaned, and since he didn't push Carey away, Carey continued. He could see Sage wiggling on top of Reece, and he could easily imagine how that felt. He wanted to feel it too, and he knew that eventually, he would. But this time, their first time, was all about Reece.

"You two are going to drive me crazy," Reece murmured.

"That's kind of the point, isn't it?" Carey asked before kissing Reece again. He didn't want Reece to speak. He wanted Reece to forget what was happening and focus on his body and how good this felt. Since this was the first time he was with a guy, let alone two of them, he deserved to feel cherished, and Carey knew how to make that happen. It would be even easier with Sage's cooperation, and Sage seemed to be particularly enthusiastic about that.

Sage wiggled his way down Reece's body, spreading himself between Reece's legs, his lips hovering above Reece's cock. He looked up at Reece, and Reece looked down at him.

Carey wasn't jealous. Reece and Sage shared a bond he didn't have a place in, and that was okay. For them, this was a huge step forward in their relationship, and Carey was grateful and honored to be a part of it.

He followed suit, moving down Reece's body, leaving a path of kisses and light bites. He didn't mark Reece's skin, even though he wanted to. He needed to ask Reece about it first. He didn't want to embarrass Reece, and getting naked in front of people was almost a guarantee when you were a shifter.

Then he and Sage were nose to nose, Reece's cock hovering between them.

Carey looked up at Reece, who swallowed heavily, and stuck his tongue out to lick the tip of Reece's cock. Sage grinned and followed his lead, kissing down the sensitive skin. Together, they focused on giving Reece the best blowjob he'd ever had. Carey knew exactly what it felt to have two guys focus on your junk, and it was heaven. He made sure to put all the tricks he'd learned over the years into it, using his tongue, his lips, and even his teeth a few times. Reece didn't seem to mind, if his moans and groans were anything to go by.

But he wasn't the only guy involved. Without taking his lips away from Reece — and it was a small miracle that Carey managed to do this — Carey wiggled until he was on his side and inched closer to Sage. He gently turned Sage so they were facing each other, their feet hanging off the bed, their heads resting on Reece's thighs. Then he reached between them and wrapped his hand around both their cocks.

Sage jerked, his eyes going wide. He stopped sucking on the head of Reece's cock

Carey arched a brow, tilting his head until he understood that he should continue.

And continue he did. Once the surprise passed, he got back into it, enthusiastically.

It made Carey smile, and he was grateful that Sage was the one focusing on Reece. That way, Carey could focus on both him and Sage, even though he never stopped licking Carey's cock and kissing his thighs and stomach.

It was a bit awkward, but it was also perfect, more than any first time Carey had had.

Reece came first, spurting over his stomach, and Carey winked at him as he raised his body and licked the seed. It made Reece shudder and Sage moan, and Carey wasn't surprised when the next time he pulled on their cocks, Sage came between them.

Then Carey was the only one left. He was stunned when Sage took the lead, pushing Carey to his back and settling between his legs. Reece also managed to move and kissed Carey while Sage blew him to orgasm.

Then the three of them flopped onto the bed. Carey couldn't have moved even he'd needed to, and thankfully, he didn't. He was where he wanted and was supposed to be. He was where he would be for the rest of his life.

"That was something," Reece said.

Carey propped himself on his elbow so he could look at both his men. "You liked that? Because I'm not sure how to take your words." He was more nervous than he'd ever been, and while he didn't like it, he also knew it was normal.

Reece rolled his eyes. "Of course I liked that. How could I have not? You two are great with your tongues."

Sage made a strangled sound and slapped Reece's thigh. "That's all we're great with?"

Reece laughed, and it happened seldom enough that Carey was amazed by the sound. He wanted to hear it more often, and right then and there, he decided he would do whatever he needed to do to make that happen.

"You're good at everything. Your mouth, your tongue, your hands." Reece hesitated and looked both at Sage and Carey. "Your hearts. I'm amazed that this is going as well as it's going. I didn't think it was possible. But thank you, both of you. Thank you for pushing me and making me see that this could work. If you hadn't, I'd still be alone, and I'd be watching you from afar, envious and jealous."

This was a serious moment, but it was becoming *too* serious, and Carey wanted them to enjoy the afterglow, so he said, "Does that mean you're a creep? I mean, you like to watch. Wait, that's a great idea for the next time we have sex. We can stick you in the armchair in the corner while Sage and I have sex on the bed. What you think about that?"

Reece burst out laughing. "Sure. Why not? I guess I have a lot of things to explore with you."

And all that mattered was that it would happen with Sage and Carey.

Reece was at peace. It was weird to feel that way, like the pain in his chest that had finally faded enough for him to breathe.

He'd never thought he'd have this. He'd thought he'd have to carry his pain for the rest of his life, and while it was still present, it had shrunk enough that it could be replaced by love. Love for the two men he was in bed with. Love for Sage, and eventually, for Carey, too.

It was incredible, and while Reece still felt slightly guilty, he knew that Emily wouldn't have wanted him to feel that way. She would have wanted him to be happy. He would have wanted the same thing for her if he'd been the one who had died, and he was only now starting to realize that yes, there could be more to his life than what he'd allowed himself to have.

He knew some people wouldn't be happy. His parents would pitch a fit at the idea of him being with two men, especially if they ever found out that Sage and Carey were mates. But they would also be sad, because Reece had never told them about Emily. He'd excluded them from that part of his life, from his pain, from the help they could have given him if they'd known. And Reece was starting to realize that maybe he'd been wrong when he'd done that. He'd forced himself to carry the pain alone all these years, but maybe it would have been easier for him to heal if he'd allowed someone to help.

But all of that was a moot point now. There was no coming back from it. There was only going forward, and that was what he was doing.

He rolled his head on the pillow and looked at Sage and Carey. They were curled around each other, both of them asleep.

They were also both touching him. Even though they shared the mate bond, Reece didn't feel excluded. If anything, he felt like they were doing their best to include him in their relationship, and it humbled him. It would have been so easy for both of them to ignore him. It would no doubt have been easier for their bond if he hadn't been in their life. But he was, and neither of them had tried to push him away.

Instead, they'd given him time to wrap his mind around was what was happening. They'd given him time to understand his feelings and to accept that yes, he wanted Sage, and that since it meant that Carey would be right there with him, he would have to accept Carey, too. He hadn't been sure it would work, but now he knew it could. It was an odd arrangement, but who cared? Reece certainly didn't. Now that he'd finally gotten over his hesitancy, he could see that this would be good for the three of them. Even the people who wouldn't like it would have to admit it.

He was starting to change. He was letting go of the pain and the memories. That could only be good for him, and he couldn't wait to see what the future would be like. Carey might be the phoenix shifter, but it was Reece who was rising from the ashes of his old life, the life he'd forced on himself, and getting ready to start a new one.

He closed his eyes. It was the first time he'd had sex with a man, let alone two, and he couldn't wait to do it again. Carey and Sage had focused on him, something he hadn't expected, and it had overwhelmed him, but in a good way. If he thought about it, his entire body tingled, and his cock thickened. Now wasn't the moment, though. He wasn't about to wake either Carey or Sage. He didn't want anything from them but what they were already giving him by being in bed with him.

They were touching him, Sage's arm around his waist, Carey's hand possessively holding his thigh. He wouldn't be able to move away from the bed without them noticing, and he suspected that was why they had fallen asleep in this position.

But he wasn't going anywhere, and one day soon, they would realize that. They would stop being afraid, and Reece would work toward that goal.

Reece wasn't sure what jerked him awake, but he looked around the bedroom, wondering what was wrong. Because something was wrong. He was sure of it. But Sage and Carey were still in bed with him, asleep, although Carey's eyes were fluttering open.

Then Reece heard it again. Someone was knocking on the door — or rather, it sounded like they were trying to kick the door down.

Reece jumped out of bed just as Carey opened his eyes.

They looked at each other, and Carey nodded, slipping away from Sage, leaving him in bed while he and Reece went downstairs. Reece had no idea what was happening, but it couldn't be a good thing to have someone pound on Sage's door in the middle of the night.

It wasn't. He opened the door and found himself facing Camden. Camden looked him up and down, and his eyes widened, especially when he caught sight of Carey behind Reece. "You're naked."

Reece realized that yes, he was, and so was Carey. Before he could say anything, Carey pushed past him, seemingly uncaring that he was naked in front of a guy who wasn't part of their relationship. "What happened?" he asked.

Reece had never heard him like that. Carey always sounded carefree and happy. He was all business now, though. He was serious and focused, and Reece was a bit in awe. There was so much to discover about Carey, much more than he'd thought in the beginning. He couldn't wait to learn Carey, but he wished it wasn't this way.

"Is Toby here?" Camden asked.

"No. I haven't seen him in a while. He went to work with Naila earlier."

But he should have been home now. It was the middle of the night.

"He's not home. He wasn't when I came back. It took me a bit to realize that because I was trying not to wake him up. I thought he was asleep."

"Shit. He said he wasn't going anywhere but at Naila's, and Lennox went with him. You're sure he's not home?"

Camden glared at him. "Of course I'm sure. Do you think I wouldn't have made sure of it before coming here?" His expression twisted with pain. "Please. I need you to find him."

"Of course. Give me one minute. I just need to throw on some clothes."

Carey turned around, and Reece followed him up the stairs, leaving the door open for Camden to come in — or not. They were going to be out of the house soon anyway.

Carey barged into the bedroom, jerking Sage awake. He didn't even look at Sage, though, making a beeline for his clothes instead.

Reece knew he was angry and felt guilty. Reece couldn't allow him to feel that way, though. He grabbed Carey's arm and pulled him back before Carey could dress. He forced Carey to look at him, even when Carey tried to jerk back.

"It wasn't your fault," he said.

Carey turned his wide eyes toward Reece.

Reece could see the pain in them.

"It was. I'm here to protect him. I failed."

Reece shook his head. "You can't be with him twenty-four. Camden didn't expect you to do that. You and Lennox are here to protect Toby and Sam, and to protect the pack, but you also have to live your own life. Camden won't blame you for what happened."

Carey raked a hand through his already messy hair. "But I do. I should have been there with him instead of here."

Reece crossed his arms over his chest and scowled at him. "You could have, sure. But instead, you were with Sage and me. You regret it?"

Carey opened his mouth, snapped it shut, then closed his eyes and shook his head. "I can never regret what happened between us last night. That doesn't change the fact that I failed, though." He opened his eyes and looked at Reece. "I should have protected him."

"Sure, you should have. But so should Lennox and Camden. Their main goal in life right now is to protect Toby and Sam, but they failed, too. What else could you have done? You cleared this date with Camden. I know you did. You also talked to Toby and Lennox, didn't you? You made sure that it was okay with them if you took the night off."

"Of course I did."

"And what did Toby have to say about that?"

"He told me to go out and to make the two of you happy. He told me he was going to work and go home. I thought he'd be safe."

"Everyone thought he would be. No one expected this to happen. We thought that after the envoy left, the Springfield pack would leave us alone. It's a miracle you're still here, because you're going to be able to help us find Toby. Don't blame yourself for something you couldn't have changed. Instead, work toward getting Toby back. That's all everyone wants right now. No one is angry with you, and no one blames you. But Camden certainly will if you don't do something."

Carey stood up straighter. "You're right. I can't change the past, but I can change the future. I'll find him. Lennox and I will."

Reece had no doubt that would happen. Carey was stubborn. He would do anything to find Toby and bring him home, and Reece felt sorry for the people who would stand in his way.

CHAPTER EIGHT

Sage was grateful that no one suggested he stay home. He wouldn't have. Toby was his friend, and more importantly, he was Sam's brother and Camden's mate. He was the alpha mate, and they needed to bring him home safely.

As soon as he realized what was happening, he threw on some clothes. Then he followed Reece and Carey out of the house, where they joined Camden on the porch. He knew he wouldn't be useful in this situation, but he needed to be there. He needed to know what was happening before he went crazy.

"Do we have any idea when he was taken or where?" Carey asked.

Sage blinked at his question. He hadn't thought about that. Had someone snuck into pack territory? It wouldn't be unheard of. The pack was small, and it wasn't gated or anything like that. People were allowed to go back and forth, and they'd never needed to be protected that way. Maybe that should change, though. With the Springfield pack threatening them and possibly taking Toby, they would need to find a way to protect all the pack members.

But first, they needed to find Toby.

Who had taken him? The only thing that made sense was that the Springfield pack was still trying to obtain one of the unicorn shifters. Sage understood why they were doing it, of course. Unicorn shifters were precious. Sage himself had been used because of his gift, and being an empath wasn't anything special. It was useful when you had business meetings and stuff like that, but that was about it. On the other hand, unicorn shifters could heal, and that *was* special. It was so special that apparently the Springfield pack had been okay with putting themselves against two phoenix shifters and risking a war between packs.

Carey and Lennox were going to burn the world down to get Toby back, and while it was reassuring to know that they were doing something, it was also a bit terrifying. Sage knew Carey pretty well by now, and he knew that sometimes he lost control of his emotions. That could make things dangerous, especially since he could create fire out of nowhere.

"They probably snuck in. Or maybe they managed to get him out of pack territory somehow," Camden said. His voice was constricted. Sage could feel the fear pouring out of him, and it was hard to focus on anything else, but he forced himself to.

He knew Camden was afraid. They all were. He didn't have to read anyone's emotions to be aware of that.

"He wouldn't have followed anyone, especially not someone he didn't know," Sage pointed out.

"That's true. He knew how dangerous the Springfield pack was. I'm ready to bet that someone snuck in," Carey agreed. "Was the house broken into?"

"Not that I noticed, but I didn't check the windows and doors. When I didn't find him in bed and he didn't answer when I called out for him, I went over the house. Then I came to talk to Sam and Sage. I was hoping that maybe . . ." He shook himself. "But he wasn't with Sage, obviously, nor with Sam."

"Where is Sam?" Sage asked. His best friend had to be terrified, and while Sage wasn't looking forward to having to add that second hand feeling to his own fear, he needed to be there for Sam.

"He was talking about going out to the house he shared

with Toby and their parents, just in case Toby went there and fell asleep or something. He and Frederic are probably on their way there."

"But you don't think Toby is there."

Camden shook his head. "I don't. He would have left me a note if he went there, and he usually avoids going in the dark. The place is a mess, and he wouldn't want to hurt himself. No. I think that the Springfield pack somehow managed to sneak in without anyone noticing them and grabbed him."

"Why him instead of Sam? This is even worse. I mean, Toby is the alpha mate. I don't know the Springfield pack, but it's hard to believe they would have done something like that." Because it was a declaration of war, and now the Rosewood pack would be in their right to strike and destroy the Springfield pack.

Sage knew that probably wouldn't happen. The Rosewood pack was tiny, especially next to the Springfield pack. But they had Carey and Lennox, and that meant that if they wanted, they could probably burn the Springfield pack to the ground. Camden wasn't the kind of guy who would do something like that, but right now, he might not be thinking entirely straight. No one would stop him if that was what he decided to do. Someone had taken his mate, and that someone needed to pay. Everyone would understand that, and while they might not agree, they *would* agree that Camden was in his right.

Sage hoped it wouldn't come down to that. He wanted to get Toby back, of course, and he wanted Toby to be safe and for the Springfield pack to leave them alone, but killing women and children wouldn't help. Killing men who had nothing to do with this wouldn't, either. They needed to find Toby without hurting anyone, and maybe once they found the people responsible for this, they could find a good punishment for them.

"Sam was home today," Camden explained. "He wasn't feeling well, so he didn't go to Naila's."

"But Toby did," Carey said.

"Yes. I think he was probably snatched on his way home. It would make more sense than have someone sneak into the house, especially since it was locked, and Naila would have called me if Toby had never arrived, so we know he was with her then left. If it were me, I would have waited for him in the forest. It would have been far enough away from the pack so no one would hear anything."

"That means they know the pack and the territory," Carey pointed out.

Camden nodded. "Probably. Pack territory isn't big. It wouldn't be hard for anyone to find out who lived where, and even the members' routines." He raked a hand through his hair just as they got to his house. "We need to find him. After everything he's been through, I can't leave him in the hands of the Springfield pack. I won't allow them to use him the way that gang did. He's suffered enough."

To Sage's relief and surprise, Reece caught Camden's arm. He put both his hands on Camden's shoulders and waited for Camden to look at him before speaking. "We'll find him," he said, his voice full of promises. "I don't know how long it's going to take us, or how hard it's going to be, but we'll find him. He's your mate, and that's more important than any-thing else. We all want you to be happy, and we all want him to be home. I know it's useless to say this, but you need to relax and think straight. You need to think like an alpha, be-cause that's what you are. Stop freaking out. I know it's hard. But Toby is strong. He wouldn't be your mate if he weren't."

Camden rubbed his face, and his shoulders slumped. "I know you're right. But it's hard. I'm terrified. What if I never get him back? What if he gets hurt?"

"They need him," Sage said, getting everyone's attention.

He shuffled his feet, uncomfortable with that, but he needed to finish his thought. "They need a healer, right? That's why they were after unicorn shifters. It wouldn't be good for them to hurt him, because he wouldn't be able to heal anyone. I'm wondering if maybe someone high up in the pack hierarchy is hurt or something like that. They were very insistent on having a unicorn shifter, and even though they backed off for a bit, now they've snatched Toby. There's a sense of urgency in this, and I don't think they can afford to hurt him."

Camden nodded. "You're right. There has to be a reason they need him so badly, and we have to find that reason."

Sage hoped he wasn't wrong. Unicorn shifters were precious, as what had happened to Toby and Sam's family showed. People were ready to do just about anything to have one in their pack. Maybe Sage was wildly off, but he hoped that Toby was okay.

He had to be. Sage couldn't lose one of his friends, not when his life was finally coming together.

Carey was guilty. It didn't matter what Reece said, Carey was guilty of not doing his job and putting Toby in danger.

Toby shouldn't have been going around the forest on his own. He should have been with Lennox, and Carey still didn't know what had happened to Lennox. Something had to have happened, since he hadn't been with Toby.

He knew Toby had been planning to work with the healer. He hadn't thought about it much, though. It was routine. Carey had been focused on his date with Reece and Sage, and everything else had flown right out the window. And now Toby was missing.

He, Reece, and Sage followed Camden into the house. Every light seemed to be on, maybe to make sure the Toby wasn't there, but no one came to meet them. Toby wasn't here, and Carey couldn't help but feel guilty about it.

The door opened just as they closed it. Lennox stepped in, and Carey rounded against his brother. "Where the fuck were you?" he snapped.

Lennox took a step back, clearly startled, then crossed his arms over his chest and schooled his expression. Now Carey couldn't tell what he was thinking or feeling. They were twins, though, and Carey knew his brother better than anyone.

"What the fuck do you want?" Lennox asked, his voice deceptively calm.

"You knew I wouldn't be here tonight. Why weren't you with Toby?"

"I was."

Carey threw his hands in the air. "Clearly, you weren't."

"I was," Lennox repeated. "I went with him to Naila's, and I stayed there while they worked together. Then, we started walking home."

"Where is he, then?"

"We were about halfway home when he realized he'd forgotten his phone at Naila's house. He went back to get it. He told me to go ahead because he knew I had something planned. I didn't think it would be a problem since we were in pack territory, and the Springfield pack never encroached, and they've been quiet since Carey almost burned their envoy to ashes."

Carey rubbed his eyes. He knew he shouldn't yell at his brother. No matter what Lennox had done, Carey had done just the same thing. Both of them were at fault here, and it wouldn't be useful to anyone to end up in a screaming match.

"Okay, so someone was watching you. They probably took advantage as soon as you left. Do we know if Toby managed to get back to Naila's?"

He looked at Camden as he spoke, and Camden shook his

head.

"I didn't even know about any of this. I'm going to call her and ask."

Carey nodded. At least this way, Camden would have something to do, and he might not freak out as badly as already was. Carey needed to stop freaking out, too, though. He wouldn't help anyone by yelling and accusing. The time for that would come later, once they had Toby back.

Carey couldn't even imagine what Camden would do if Toby was hurt. Camden would make sure that the people who'd been in charge of keeping him safe would know what he thought. He might even kick Lennox and Carey out of the pack, and if that happened, Carey didn't know what he'd do. Could he leave Sage and Reece behind? Or would they come with him? He would never ask that of them, but he couldn't imagine the rest of his life without them, even though he'd only been in Rosewood for a few months.

It had been a few months of bliss, and he didn't want to give that up. Maybe if he found Toby, Camden would be more lenient. Maybe he would let Lennox and Carey stay.

That meant that Carey had to find Toby as soon as possible, and hopefully, unhurt.

"We need to decide what to do," Lennox said. He was looking at Carey, and while he didn't look angry, Carey knew he was. Carey was going to have to apologize to his brother and a bunch of other people once this was over.

He would. "What you mean?"

"The Springfield pack is much bigger. They would win in an outright fight, and you and I both know it. We can't just go there with a bunch of people and demand they give Toby back, especially since we have no proof they're the ones who took him."

"What did you have in mind, then?"

Lennox stared at Carey, and Carey knew what he was

thinking about. Still, he let Lennox say it out loud because he didn't want his boyfriends to kill him.

"We should go, the two of us. *Just* the two of us."

That was what Carey had been thinking. He wasn't surprised when Sage protested, though. "The two of you are not going anywhere. What the fuck are you thinking? You can't put yourself in danger that way."

It was sweet. It was *adorable*. Even though Carey and Lennox hadn't done their job and had allowed one of Sage's best friends to be taken, he was still trying to protect them. God, Carey loved that man. He loved Sage and Reece, and he never wanted to leave them.

But right now, Toby was more important.

"Think about it," Lennox said, ignoring Sage's words and still staring at Carey. "We can take care of a lot of people on our own. Besides, the Springfield pack will expect the pack to go to their territory and demand Toby be given back. They won't expect just the two of us. We can set a few fires and distract most of the pack, and once that's done, we can sneak in and find Toby."

Carey nibbled on his lower lip. Usually, their presence was enough of a deterrent to keep people from attacking. They couldn't be killed. What their mother had done had needed a specific type of poison, and it was extremely rare. Even if someone shot at them or attacked them, they wouldn't die. They were phoenix shifters, and they would regenerate.

That meant that they had yet another advantage, even though Carey hated regenerating. It was a pain in the ass, and he didn't like being covered in ashes. But he couldn't deny that Lennox was right. It made sense. It wouldn't put anyone in danger, and Carey and Lennox could defend themselves better than most pack members.

"Sage is right," Reece snapped. "You can't go there halfcocked. We need to think about this and talk. We need to make sure everyone is on the same track."

"This is what we have to do," Carey said. He prayed that his boyfriend would understand. He prayed that they wouldn't hate him by the end of the night. But if they did, he would have to deal with it. "It was our job to keep Toby safe, and we failed. But we can get him back, and that's what we're going to do."

"You're not going anywhere before you speak to me," Camden said as he stepped back into the entrance. He was putting his phone back into his pocket, and he shook his head. "Naila doesn't know where he is, but he did come back to her house to grab his phone. That's the last time she saw him, though."

So Toby had been taken between Naila's house and the one he shared with Camden. He'd been taken in pack territory.

That meant that the Springfield pack had taken yet one more step toward war, and Carey didn't like that. He didn't want Reece and Sage to be in danger.

He and Lennox would have to take care of this. It didn't matter if something happened to them — and he knew nothing would. He needed to keep the pack safe, and the best way to do that was to keep the pack out of the negotiations to get Toby back.

Carey cracked his knuckles. "Lennox and I are going. We'll get Toby back. I promise." He hoped he wouldn't have to break that promise. He would certainly do everything he could to make sure he kept it.

"You are *not* going alone."

Reece could have kissed Camden for laying down the law. He knew Carey would have rushed into danger without thinking twice about it if it meant bringing Toby home, but he couldn't do that. He wasn't alone anymore. He didn't just have Lennox to think about. Now he had Reece and Sage, and he needed to keep them in mind. He needed to remember that they were part of his life and that he was part of theirs.

Reece wasn't about to allow the idiot to get himself killed just after he'd finally accepted that he was falling in love with him and that he wanted both Carey and Sage in his life, dammit.

Carey crossed his arms over his chest. "Taking anyone else with us will put them in danger."

Camden looked like he wanted to strangle Carey, and Reece understood that instinct. He wanted to do pretty much the same thing. "I don't care. I won't be happy if I get Toby back, but you and Lennox get killed in the process. Toby wouldn't be happy about that. He'd feel guilty, and that's the last thing I want. You're going, but not alone."

"You can't come with us."

Camden arched a brow. "Really? I thought I was the alpha."

"Exactly. Which means you're going to be a target."

"But he has to come, because Toby is his mate and because he's the alpha," Lennox said. His voice was quiet and settled, as it always was. He almost sounded like nothing important was happening, but Reece knew Lennox was taking this as hard as Carey. They took their job very seriously, and Toby's disappearance meant they hadn't been doing it. There would be no convincing them otherwise.

"He's right," Camden agreed. "I'm going with you, whether you like it or not. What the Springfield pack did is unacceptable, and I'm going to tell them exactly that. Besides, just like you pointed out, you and Lennox are more than able to protect me and take care of the Springfield pack if you need to."

Carey huffed. "Fine. But no one else."

"I'm coming, too," Reece said. He suspected Frederic

would also want to come. Maybe even Sam, although that would put him in danger, and they couldn't allow that.

It was exactly what the Springfield pack wanted. They wanted the unicorn shifters, and apparently, they were ready to do just about anything to get their hands on them. If Camden managed to take Toby back, they wouldn't hesitate to grab Sam if they had the chance.

Carey slowly turned to look at Reece. "I'm sorry?"

Reece knew he had a fight on his hands, and he didn't care. "Everyone in the pack is trained to fight. We don't have guards because we're so small, which means that all of us help to protect the pack. We all failed when Toby was taken, and I want to go with you."

"Nope. No way."

Reece knew Carey was going to be pissed, but he didn't care. "As Camden pointed out, you're not the alpha. He is. He's also a friend, as is Toby. I'm not letting the three of you go alone, and I know I'm not the only one who will want to come with you." But Frederic needed to rush back, because otherwise, they were going to leave without him. They needed to get to the Springfield pack, and they needed to get there soon.

Reece didn't think the Springfield pack would hurt Toby, but they had to know that Rosewood would come after them. It meant they might move him, at least in the beginning, just to make sure the Rosewood pack wouldn't be able to find him.

"This is nuts," Carey said, throwing his hands in the air. "Why do you all want to get yourself killed?"

"They won't kill us," Reece said. He was sure about that.

Carey pointed a finger at him. "Only because me and Lennox will make sure they don't. But the more people we have to think of, the less efficient we will be."

"And again, all the pack members are trained to fight. I can

111

take care of myself. You focus on the Springfield pack and on finding Toby. I'll stay with Camden." He turned to Camden. "And yes, I know you can take care of yourself. That's not what I meant. You're going to be distracted, because you'll know that Toby is there. I want to keep an eye on you and make sure no one takes advantage of that. That's all. I won't start a fight with anyone, but I'll be ready to defend myself and you if they do."

"I want to come, too," Sage said

Reece had expected that, too. "You need to stay here."

Sage's eyes narrowed, and he crossed his arms over his chest. He looked like he was about to start yelling.

Reece prepared himself for the onslaught of words.

"Why should I stay here? Is it because I'm smaller? Because I'm not a predator? You think I can't defend myself?"

"I know you can defend yourself if you need to. But think about it. Carey and I need to be focused on getting Toby back and on protecting Camden. Do you know what's going to happen if you come with us? We'll be distracted. We'll focus on you instead of them, and that won't work. Eventually, someone is going to notice, and they'll take advantage of the feelings Carey and I have for you. We need to avoid that." Reece reached for Sage, and he was relieved when Sage didn't move away. He took one of Sage's hands and dragged him close, wrapping his arms around him. "Please. Carey and I need to know you're safe. It's the only way we'll be able to focus on getting Toby back, and I know you want that as much as we do."

Reece was only half surprised when Carey stepped closer, too. He'd expected Carey to hold onto his anger, but instead, Carey pulled both of them into his arms. "He's right," he murmured. "I've never had someone to think of when I fought, you know? I've never had anyone waiting for me at home. I think that's part of why I always throw myself in danger, but it's different now. If I know I have you to come back home to, I'll be extra careful. And Reece is right about the fact that I'll be distracted if you're there. I know you want to come, and I love you for that. I love you for how much you care about Toby and for the way you want to help. But coming with us will complicate things instead of helping."

Sage's breath hitched.

Reece wished he could get the same words past his own lips, but he couldn't. He couldn't tell Sage he loved him and not say the same to Carey. It wouldn't be fair.

Carey tilted his head and looked at Reece. "And I love you too, you dumbass stubborn man. I hope you know what you're doing, because I won't be able to focus on you, either. It's going to be hell, though. I'll hold you responsible if anything happens to you, and I'll resuscitate you only to kill you again."

That startled a laugh out of Reece. "You know that's not possible."

"I'll find a way. Everything is possible if I want it enough."

Camden cleared his throat. "I know this isn't easy on anyone, but we need to go."

He was right, and after kissing Sage, Reece took a step back. Carey stayed close to Sage, though, and tilted Sage's face so Sage would look him in the eyes. "I'll keep Reece safe. I promise. I care about you and Reece more than I've ever cared about anyone but Lennox. I'm not going to lose one of you while I retrieve Toby. You'll see. We'll be back soon, and Reece will be okay."

Sage nodded. "I know. But I'm scared."

Reece was, too, and he knew Sage could feel it. He didn't say anything. He didn't have to. Instead, he kissed Sage again, then he and Carey turned to face Camden. "We're ready," Reece said.

Camden was still pale, but he looked resolute. He nodded

at them. "Good. Because we're getting my mate back, and we're doing it right now."

CHAPTER NINE

They didn't try to stop them. That was the first thing that surprised Carey, and he forced himself to focus on what was happening.

Why wasn't the Springfield pack trying to stop them from entering their territory? They had guards. Carey was sure about that. He'd counted at least three of them up in the trees in the forest around them, yet none of them had even tried to talk to them. Something was going on, and Carey didn't know what it was. He hated not knowing what was happening.

"Something's up," Lennox murmured.

Carey nodded. He didn't have to say anything for Lennox to understand that he shared that opinion. Something was going on, and they were about to find out what it was.

Apparently, Camden knew where the alpha house was. He might have spent some time with the Springfield pack in the past, but Carey thought it was weird. As far as he knew, the Springfield pack had always been an antagonist of the Rosewood pack, even though the Rosewood pack was so small. He wasn't sure what was going on, but he should have asked Camden for more details before they came.

It was too late now, though.

Carey, Lennox, Reece, and Frederic hopped out of the cars and followed Camden. Camden stopped in front of a large house made mostly of wood that wouldn't have looked out of place in the middle of the mountains and crossed his arms over his chest.

Then he waited.

Carey had no idea how this worked. There weren't enough phoenix shifters in the world for them to fight. If they wanted to keep their species alive, they couldn't afford it.

Was Camden going to do something to the alpha? Was he going to threaten him, or maybe fight him for Toby's honor, or whatever? This was interesting, yet Carey found that he couldn't stop worrying about Reece. Reece, who was as stubborn as Carey. Reece, who'd insisted on coming, and who was distracting Carey, even though he'd told Carey he didn't need him to think about him. How was Carey supposed to do that? No matter how well Reece could fight, this still wasn't his job. It was Carey's.

The door opened, and a man stepped out. He had to be in his mid-fifties. While his stomach was on the soft side, his muscles still bunched under his t-shirt and pants as he stepped out of the house and walked down the porch steps. His hair was almost entirely white, and he had a mustache.

Why did the bad guys always have a mustache?

"Alpha Cook. What can I do for you?" he asked.

"You can give me back my mate," Camden stopped. He sounded angry, and Carey knew the man in front of them had noticed Camden didn't use his honorific title of alpha.

The alpha's eyes widened slightly. That was the only sign that he was surprised. "I'm afraid I don't understand."

"You don't understand. You don't understand that my mate has disappeared. Someone took him, and I know it was you. You know the kind of offense this is. If you give me Toby back right now, without a scratch on his body, I won't order my phoenix shifters to burn the pack to the ground."

Normally, Carey would have bristled at being ordered to do anything. He kind of did, but he knew where Camden was coming from. Besides, Camden was now his alpha, his and Lennox's. They'd made it official with Douglas, since there was no way Carey was ever leaving Rosewood. Douglas hadn't been happy, but Carey and Lennox weren't his prisoners. They were allowed to move anywhere they wanted, and that was what they'd done.

So yes, Camden was Carey's alpha, and if he ordered him to, Carey *would* burn this place to the ground. He wouldn't even hesitate. Springfield had taken the first step. They were the ones who'd started this, and Carey and Lennox would be the one to finish it if necessary.

"Again, I'm not sure what you're talking about."

Camden frowned. "I just told you. Toby is gone, and I know it was you."

The alpha shook his head. "No, it wasn't."

"You wanted him. You wanted him and Sam because they're unicorn shifters. Don't think I forgot that you sent that envoy a few months ago."

The alpha moved closer, and Carey and Lennox took a step closer to Camden. The alpha hesitated, but Carey was surprised to see that he still came to stand in front of Camden — within reach of Carey and Lennox. That meant that they could set him on fire without a second thought, and there was nothing he would be able to do against it.

Of course, they would have been able to do the same even if he'd been on his porch, but still.

"I know what I did. I did send John to talk to you because I wanted one of the unicorn shifters, and yes, I gave you an ultimatum. I shouldn't have. But you know how rare and important unicorn shifters are. I just wanted one of them for my pack. I know you can understand that."

"What I know is that you didn't take no for an answer," Camden said, his voice hard.

"Would you have?"

"Yes. Because no one owes my pack anything. I know that I can't force anyone to move in with us and do what I tell them. Every single member of my pack is free to go whenever they want. I'll never force anyone of them into anything, just like my father wouldn't have. Obviously, I can't say the same about the Springfield pack."

Carey wondered if the alpha was offended. If he was, he didn't show it, but that wasn't surprising. "You're right, once again. I'll admit that in the past few years, I allowed things to happen that I shouldn't have. I'm sorry about that. But I promise you, I don't have your mate. I would never kidnap an alpha mate. I would never kidnap anyone, period. But especially not your mate. You would be in your right to start a war between our packs, and since you have phoenix shifters, the Springfield pack would disappear. I'm not about to risk that, so I didn't take your mate. I promise."

Carey's first instinct was to think that the man was lying, but he sounded truthful. Carey wasn't sure what to make of that. Maybe they should have brought Sage with them after all. He would probably have been able to tell them if the man was lying.

"I want to search your territory," Camden said. Carey was relieved he wouldn't take this man's words.

"Of course. I have nothing against that. If your mate really is here, it's not because I ordered it. Someone acted without my knowledge, and they'll need to pay for what they did."

Carey's fingers itched with the need to set something on fire, to give this alpha a warning of what would happen to him if he was lying. He didn't, though. He wasn't about to start a war. He didn't care that he and Lennox could win it, he didn't want to hurt anyone. He just wanted to go back home to his boyfriends.

Their little group moved toward the house, but before they could go far, a door slammed in the distance. There was a scream, and Carey tensed. He and Lennox placed themselves between Camden and the direction from which the scream had come, then waited to see what was happening.

When the person screaming came into view, it was nothing like what Carey had expected.

"I'm going to kill you!" Toby yelled. A man about his height was pushing him toward Camden, but Toby was fighting against him, looking over his shoulder at someone else and trying to get to them.

The envoy.

The man was sporting a bloody nose, and he looked like he'd had the shit kicked out of him. Carey had no idea what was happening, and that meant he didn't know what to do. He was entirely lost, and he looked at Camden for guidance.

Of course, Camden didn't say anything because he rushed to Toby instead.

"Toby, thank God. You're okay."

The man who'd been pushing Toby toward them stopped and took a step back, and Toby almost rushed to the envoy. Camden got to Toby first, though, and he grabbed his arm, pulling him close and hugging him.

"Let me go," Toby protested. "I'm going to kick his furry ass to hell and back."

"What happened?"

"What happened is that I didn't get to hit him long enough."

Carey laughed. He couldn't help it. He knew they weren't out of the woods yet, but this was hilarious. The envoy looked like he'd gone through a few rounds with a professional fighter, but Toby had clearly been the one to kick his ass.

"Toby?" the Springfield field pack alpha said.

Toby glared at him. "Are you the guy in charge here? Because let me tell you, you're not doing a good job." He pointed at the envoy. "He kidnapped me. He came into my territory and took me."

The alpha's expression hardened. "John?" he called out.

"Don't you *John* him. He's an asshole. He wanted revenge.

He thought your pack would be able to squash ours. He thought that maybe he could distract our phoenix shifters and take advantage of that."

The corner of the alpha's lips curled. "But you put a stop to that."

"Damn right, I did. I kicked his ass, and I'm going to do it again if you don't do anything."

"Trust me. He will wish you were still hitting him when I'm be done with him." The alpha turned to Camden. "I'm sorry this happened, and I assure you, I didn't know anything about it. John acted on his own, and he'll pay for what he did."

"That's all I ask," Camden said. "I'm taking Toby home."

"I'm not going anywhere without him," Toby said. He pointed his finger at the man who'd been pushing him away from the envoy. The man blushed and looked at his feet, but Toby wasn't done. "He was the one who untied me and made sure I was okay. It's only thanks to him that I managed to get out of the house. I'm not leaving him here, not when the pack might retaliate against him."

The alpha looked offended. "I already told you I would take care of John."

Toby turned toward him, and he looked *pissed,* so much so that Carey was grateful he wasn't in the alpha's place right now. "I don't care what you say. You're a bully. Your envoy is a bully. I won't allow any of you to hurt him. He's coming with us. As of right now, he's a Rosewood pack member, and you have nothing to say about that."

The alpha looked like he wanted to protest, but to Carey's surprise, he nodded. "As long as he's okay with that, of course."

They all turned to look at the man again. Carey was pretty sure he was a wolf shifter, but there was no way for him to tell at a distance. To his surprise, the man nodded. "I'd like that," he murmured.

Toby grinned triumphantly. "Good. Come on. We're going home."

Carey wrinkled his nose. "Already? I didn't even get to set anything on fire," he whined.

Lennox punched him in the shoulder. "Shut it." He pushed Carey toward Toby and Camden, and Toby went.

They separated at the cars, and Lennox went with Camden, Toby, and the new guy, while Carey stuck with Reece and Frederic. Carey couldn't help but notice when his brother went ramrod straight. Carey gave him a worried glance, but Lennox wasn't even looking at him.

Instead, he was looking at the new guy, the new pack member. His eyes were wide, and he was gaping, and even though Lennox wasn't saying anything, Carey suspected he knew what had happened.

He grinned. This was going to be so much fun to watch.

YOU MAY ALSO ENJOY THE FOLLOWING FROM EXTASY BOOKS INC:

Ellery
Catherine Lievens

Excerpt

This was heaven—or rather, it would be heaven if the mosquitoes hadn't decided they needed to eat Ellery. He hoped they'd get indigestion. He hoped they died because of his blood.

He scratched his arm again and contemplated what to do next. He could go back inside, which was thankfully sans mosquitoes, but he didn't want to. He was enjoying too much being outside after spending most of the recent years locked inside the house.

The entire pride had been stuck inside, and it hadn't been easy or fun. They had been allowed outside to deal with a small patch of vegetables in the garden, but even that source of food hadn't been enough for the entire pride. But Alpha Carter had been convinced that this was the best way to lead the pride, and everyone had followed. He'd been the alpha. He'd known better.

Except he hadn't, and he'd almost killed the entire pride. Ellery hadn't realized it at the time, and neither had anyone else or if they had, they hadn't said anything. But now the pride was free, and it was weird getting used to this. It was strange to be able to leave the house whenever they wanted and even be encouraged to do it. The old alpha hadn't wanted them to work outside the pride. He'd wanted to be the one to provide for the pride, and he had, at least in the beginning. But now, Gal wanted all of them to find a job, and he'd been clear that he wanted them to enjoy what they would do.

That was one of the reasons Ellery was here. He wanted to find a job to help the pride. He wanted to find a job so he didn't have to stay in the house anymore. He didn't know what he could do, though.

He'd been homeschooled, like everyone in the pride, and he knew that it wasn't anywhere close to a college diploma, but it was something. He could probably find a job in town, but he hadn't yet applied for anything because he didn't know what he wanted to do with his life.

He hadn't had a life until now. He'd thought he would continue to live the way Alpha Carter had made him live — locked in the house, going crazy having to share space with so many people. The only thing that had helped Ellery deal with it was patching up the house when it needed to be, which had become more frequent as time passed. He and Liam and a few others were the main reason the house hadn't crumbled down yet, and Ellery was proud of it. He just didn't know if he wanted to make a career out of it.

And wasn't that weird? He could build himself a career. Gal would support him, even after what Ellery's father had done.

Some days, Ellery couldn't believe his dad had tried to kill Gal and had almost killed Liam in the attempt. Other days, he understood how his father had been pushed to it. He didn't agree with what his father had done, of course. He liked Liam and Gal, and even if he hadn't, he wouldn't have supported it.

Ellery would always love his father, but he couldn't

support a man who'd almost killed two people because he wanted to become the alpha, especially after seeing what being the alpha did to a person. Alpha Carter had ended up going out of his mind. He'd tried to kidnap Cooper after Cooper had left to live with his mate. That was the thing that had precipitated the situation, and it was the reason they had Gal now. Not that Ellery cared. Gal was a better alpha than Alpha Carter had ever been, and Ellery was grateful that Gal had met his mate and had decided to stay.

That didn't change what Ellery's father had done, though. Most of the pride was still looking at Ellery as if he'd had something to do with it. He hadn't. Of course not. He and Liam were friends, and they were becoming closer now that they were allowed to. But when they looked at him, people could only see what his father had done, and they didn't care that Ellery had nothing to do with it or that he would have stopped his father if he'd known.

"Here you are," a voice said, making Ellery jump.

His heart raced as he looked around, only relaxing when he saw Liam walking toward him. "What are you doing here?" he asked.

Liam grimaced and flopped onto the stone bench next to Ellery. "Running away from Sandra."

Ellery chuckled. "What did she do now?"

"I don't know. I ran before she could find me. But she has a lot of requests and she thinks I should listen to her because she's an elder. I don't think she has a lot of trust in me, or in the fact that I'm the alpha mate."

"She's not used to it. None of us are."

Liam's shoulders slumped. "I'm not used to it, either. I don't know that I'll ever get used to it, to be honest. Me, the alpha mate. Who would've thought?"

Ellery thought that Liam was going to be a great alpha mate, but he didn't tell him that. He already had and repeating it wouldn't change that fact or that Liam didn't believe him. Liam needed to trust his abilities, but he didn't yet. The time would come, though. Ellery knew it. And if Liam needed him to, he'd be right there next to him to help him face what the future held for him in the pride.

"You have to be firmer with her," he suggested.

Liam narrowed his eyes at him. "Firmer? She's going to tear my head off with her bare teeth, and I mean her human teeth, not her tiger ones."

Ellery couldn't help it—he laughed. "No, she won't. You're younger and stronger, and probably faster."

"And that's the only reason she won't hurt me? Jeesh, El. Thank you."

"No. The reason she won't hurt you is that she's afraid of the council and of being kicked out of the pride. She's demanding, but she's just trying to see if she can get a hold on you and influence you. That's what she wants. That's what most of the elders want. They want to be an important part of the pride, and they want to make decisions."

Liam scowled. "They should have become alpha, then. They could have made all the decisions, and I would be able to spend more time with my mate."

"But Gal is the alpha, and nothing is going to change that. That means you're the alpha mate. Sandra is harmless, but you need to be careful with what you tell her. She won't forget even one word. You know how she is. And she's going to use everything she remembers to her advantage, even if it's against you."

Liam sighed heavily and tilted his face toward the sky. He closed his eyes, and he basked in the sunlight, just like Ellery had done until a few minutes ago. "Being the alpha mate is so fucking hard," he muttered. "I wish I didn't have to do this."

"But then you might not have Gal, and that's not something you want to happen."

Liam opened one eye to look at Ellery. "You're right. I don't want that to happen. I'm not letting him go now that I have him."

"And things will become easier once his friend arrives,

right?"

It was the talk of the entire pride. Instead of asking one of them to become the beta, Gal had asked one of his friends. Apparently, it was fairly common for groups involved with the council. The council sent alphas and betas to the shifter groups who needed them, and they helped those groups build themselves up.

The difference was that the alphas and betas usually left once that was done, but Gal wasn't going anywhere. He'd met Liam, and he'd settled down. Most of the pride agreed that he would be a good permanent alpha. But he needed a beta, and he'd explained that while he was proud of the progress the pride was making and how its members were behaving, he didn't think that any of them could become a beta. No one had that kind of experience, and after spending so much time under the thumb of Alpha Carter and his beta, they couldn't shoulder the job and responsibilities it implied.

So he'd called someone from outside, and a lot of pride members hadn't liked it, Sandra included. Ellery was ready to bet that was why she was hounding Liam, even though there was nothing he could do about it. He might be the alpha mate, but he didn't make this kind of decision. Gal did.

Ellery reached out and patted Liam's knee. "Everything is going to be okay. You just have to stand up to her, and to anyone else with something to tell you. You're the alpha mate. You should be respected, just like Gal." Ellery knew all about losing respect, and he never wanted that to happen to Liam. It was already more than enough that he was a pariah in his own pride.

He would never wish that on anyone else, not even his worst enemy — not even Sandra.

ABOUT THE AUTHOR

Catherine is the creator of several series, most of them para-normal, including the Whitedell Pride Series and the Gillham Pack Series. While she graduated in translation, she decided to go the writer's way because it was more fun to create her own stories and characters.

She's been living in Italy for more than twenty years, but she's a daughter of the North—Belgium to be precise—and she misses it so much that she's already planning to move back.

She loves pizza—probably too much—her son, her pets, and of course, books. She sneaks some reading time into her schedule every time she has five minutes free from writing, demands from her various pets and son, and lastly, house-work.

Connect with her:

lievens.catherine@gmail.com
BookBub
Website
Facebook
Facebook Group
Twitter
Newsletter